Amy Peppercorn
Living the Dream

John [illegible] partner in the southeast of En[illegible]usic of all different types, and enjoys playing squash and generally training to keep fit.

John has two children, a girl and a boy, both of whom have been instrumental in the development of his early stories for young people. He likes to draw ideas and inspiration from all aspects of life, especially from the people he meets. That's what happened when he met Amy Peppercorn.

Why not contact Amy?
www.amypeppercorn.com

Also by John Brindley

Amy Peppercorn: Starry-eyed and Screaming
Changing Emma
Rhino Boy
The Terrible Quin

Amy Peppercorn
Living the Dream

John Brindley

Dolphin Paperbacks

First published in Great Britain in 2004
as a Dolphin paperback
by Orion Children's Books
a division of the Orion Publishing Group Ltd
Orion House
5 Upper St Martin's Lane
London WC2H 9EA

A catalogue record for this book
is available from the British Library

Typeset at The Spartan Press Ltd,
Lymington, Hants

Printed in Great Britain by
Clays Ltd, St Ives plc

ISBN 1 84255 242 2

One

I've never told anyone this before, but I'll tell you: I'd have hated not to go on with it. If Beccs hadn't wanted me to continue, I would have given it all up – the singing, the money, the fame, everything; but I know I'd always have wanted to find out what would have happened. Well, I have found out, because Beccs wanted me to do it. So I can tell you.

Beccs was still my best friend. Without that, without her, I don't think I could have gone through with it. Hers was the only opinion I cared about, at the time. Even my mother seemed to abandon her principles in the excitement and hysteria of what was happening to me. My dad was mad for it, right from the start. As for Raymond Raymond, principal A and R man at Solar Records, and now my manager with a five-year contract that seems to have control over everything I do and say and think and feel – well, what could you expect of Ray Ray? 'Got to be!' he'd rattle out like a machine gun going off accidentally. 'Got to be! Right for it! Dead right for it!'

'Dead right for it,' my dad chanted, happily up to his elbows in the drama of our kitchen sink, with my twin baby sisters, Georgie and Jo, suspended from his braces.

'I hope you're right,' my mum worried, but soon shuffled off caution in the excitement of seeing her eldest daughter's tearful face on the front pages of the kind of papers she had always despised. 'You are right,' she too recited, falling in line with my dad and my manager, the orchestrator of my very life. Even my meticulous and intelligent mum couldn't resist Ray Ray's most concentrated laser beam.

'Got to be! Right for it! Dead right for it!'

But I didn't feel right for it. I felt like a fraud. If my best friend Beccs Bradley hadn't told me it was all right, then it wouldn't have been all right. Okay, I was some kind of star, an overnight sensation, but my friend Geoffrey Fryer had been killed in a joy-riding accident with Ben Lyons. What was any success of mine, compared to Geoff's whole life lost? And Ben, such a talented, tormented person, was on remand: Ben, who had kissed me, only once, but who was more special to me than he could have ever known through that single, half-missed kiss.

Our band, Car Crime, Ben's band, had broken up, smashing headlong into a metal post, but I was a star. Just me, on my own. Beccs had to try to make it work for me. Her cousin, Kirsty, tried to bring out the wrong in it, trying to blame me for everything, but Beccs would make it all right. 'We have to give Courtney Schaeffer a run for her money,' Beccs said. 'Courtney's a pop star, but she doesn't have half your talent, or a voice anywhere near as good as yours.'

I loved Beccs. She alone, the things she said, was a good enough reason not to throw the whole thing away, but it wasn't enough to make it all right. It wasn't enough to make me anything other than riding high on wrongly wrought emotions, on the back of Geoff's death and everything that went with it.

Beccs was just as hurt, just as traumatised as me, but she always had a way of focussing on things. I didn't have anything in me but Geoff's dying and Ben's remand as soon as he got out of hospital after the accident. Geoffrey Fryer was gone entirely; and so, it seemed, was Ben. Beccs and I cried in each other's arms. The papers were full of wrong tears. My mum and dad had lost their minds in Ray Ray's gun-stuttering enthusiastic utterances. Geoffrey Fryer wasn't there. I couldn't get through to Ben's mobile. He'd be switched off, perhaps entirely, not yet really understanding what had happened, what he'd done. And what he'd done, he'd done to us all, a car crime that crashed into and affected or ruined so many lives.

But Beccs said I should show the world what we were made of. We were, I felt, made of completely the wrong stuff to show the world anything. My point of view swerved from one extreme to the other with every tick of Becca's mum's living-room clock. One second I was an innocent party, a bystander caught up in uncontrollable events, the next I felt as guilty as a murderer. My stardom swayed with me, adding to the weight of the clock-pendulum, swinging me from elated and nervous happiness to massive, overbearing guilt as Beccs's tears ticked with my own into the future of what we would or would not show the world.

'What does it all mean?' I asked Beccs.

'I don't know,' she whispered. 'Something, though. It has to mean something, doesn't it?'

Everything has to mean something, doesn't it? Or what is the point of anything? Beccs decided that the point was that I would say something for Geoff. For you, Geoff. Beccs allowed me to believe in a meaning, a reason and a purpose. We cried together, looking for and finding our purpose.

It was Beccs I had to thank – or blame – for my walk back through the warm streets with her to my house where the press and my parents waited frantically, with a frantic Ray Ray stuttering admonitions and obscenities in a vicious spray of invective.

'She better not. Again. It doesn't do. Not now. We need

control. You know? You know? Control? Control!' he freaked.

My mum looked at Beccs's hand in mine, noting, above everyone, how hard we held on to one another. My mum, I thought for a moment, was showing the kind of concern that understood my anguish, my friend's anguish, our shared handhold reaching for something more than all this fury of raised voice and frantic ambition. She looked at us, my mum, only until Ray Ray's greater insistence took her attention, holding it at least as tightly as I was holding Beccs's hand and she mine.

'It's gotta be control, yeah?' Ray blasted. 'Without it, nothing. With, all! Yeah? All! Everything to play for! These are big stakes. Big breaks, though. The best. The best ever. This is it. All it needs, control, yeah?'

'Yeah,' my dad said. He was being sent to collect the twins from his sister's, where they'd spent my big night last night. The press wanted the Peppercorns completely, so my dad would gather them from wherever for the family photos.

My mum was glowing with pride on a telephone red-hot from continually ringing, from continually being answered. She had to shout to be heard above Raymond Raymond barking like a guard dog at everything that threatened me or promised us success.

Nobody said anything to Beccs. Nobody said a word to her, including me. I was trying to hold on to her – trying, failing. Too many telephone calls, too many photo opportunities, too many people turning up at our little house for their own or everybody else's self-interested reasons. Beccs looked at me from the other side of the room as I was positioned in a better light, or posed shaking hands with one after another self-interested party. She looked at me across the turmoil of my success smiling simply, encouragingly; but she looked as if she was smiling into an entirely separated, untouchable place. She nodded at me across the distance rapidly expanding between us, as if to tell me to go on, even without her. I didn't want to go without her, but she nodded to me to continue.

I can't tell you what that was like. I had to carry on. I *did* carry on, as you know, because so much has happened. Some of it you might have read about. You might even have been to see me in that time – I wonder if you did? I hope you did, then when I tell you what it was like, you might begin to feel you've been there with me, at least for part of the way.

Two

I can't tell you how much I wanted to talk to Ben. I couldn't imagine what it must be like for him. I only knew that he'd be having a bad time of it – a really bad time of it. I couldn't imagine what he was going through. His mobile was off, of course, which didn't stop me texting him:

BEN. I'M THINKING OF YOU. CALL ME, IF U CAN. AMY.

There were rehearsals now, in secret locations, in studios and in people's big houses. The two old guys who'd written *The Word on the Street* between them kept showing up. We had a few trips to a studio one of them had set up in his house – some house! My whole family could have lived in one of his garages, and he had four of them. Four garages, at least as many bathrooms and an indoor swimming pool.

They'd written scores of hit songs, these two. They'd had a hand in nearly everything, involving themselves with just about every successful or semi-successful singer or boy or girl band in the last what looked like twenty years or so. Even my dad had heard of them. So had my mum.

'They're putting songs together for you?' my dad said, pounding babies Jo and Georgie up and down in their bouncy chairs like a couple of yo-yos. The little girls shrieked and kicked, trying, and occasionally succeeding in trashing another piece of furniture. That was their favourite pastime, trashing things.

'Did you hear that?' my dad said to my mum. 'Jill, did you hear that?'

By then, I had hardly been home. I'd been whisked away, my unheld hand falling by my side too far away from friends, from Beccs, from family, from my mum, who slaved over National Curriculum bureaucracy, a hot pile of form-filling from which she never seemed to miss me at all.

'Jill?' my dad, Tony, said. 'Did you hear that? McGregor and Fine are writing songs for Amy! What about that, then? They're like –'

'They wrote *The Word on the Street*, didn't they?' my mum turned and said, looking at my father.

'Did they?' he said, turning to me.

I nodded. My mum looked like every teacher I've ever known – too busy, too preoccupied, too immersed in procedures to ever really teach anybody anything.

'Poo!' my darling baby sisters decided.

'McGregor and Fine, eh?' my dad said, whistling his approval.

Mum disappeared behind the National Curriculum, fuzzily disconnected from anything. This was the first time I'd seen her properly for days. I'd been whisked away from her as she'd tried to find out what on earth had happened that night with Ben and me. With Ben and me, with Ben and Geoff. And with the police. My mum, looking at me before Ray Ray went whisking, saw something of the wild blue car chases, the siren night of epileptic crashes, fatal accidents on the other side of town, on the other side of the law. 'What happened? What on earth happened, Amy? That boy died!'

As if I didn't – as if I hadn't realised *that that boy died*! As if I never knew him or what he'd been through. As if I hadn't lain awake thinking about the fact that he'd died and I'd maybe had something to do with it, although I wasn't being questioned about it by anyone but my mother. She didn't have much of an opportunity. I seemed to belong to Solar Records now, to Raymond Raymond and to the manic arrangements and rehearsals I was immediately immersed in. Ray bustled me away from my mother's concern and my father's care. I went to be taught songs that the old guys, McGregor and Fine, churned out for me. I went to people's huge houses with indoor pools and en-suite recording studios, staying over in colossal rooms, hiding from the press until the time was deemed, by somebody else, to be right.

Half the time, in those first few days or weeks, I didn't know what was going on. To be honest, now, I can't really remember what happened or in which order the scattered, frantic events took place. All I can remember is my own confusion, swinging from elated excitement to fear, or at least extreme nervousness, with moments of blind panic and sorrow and mourning in between. I had to learn, so quickly, how to smile. There is a camera-smile, a press publicity expression that imposes, superimposes itself upon a face like mine, covering me in spotlight happiness. It's not to say I was unhappy, or that what was happening didn't excite me, but not all the time. Not every time the anonymous person doing my deciding for me sent in more cameras was I this picture of popularity, this pop-star perfect. It just wasn't always like that for me, although you wouldn't know it, looking over those old press photographs. I did a good job. I must have been pretty strong.

I was texting Ben, getting nothing back. But Beccs and I were in text contact the whole time. I had to, had to maintain contact with her. I needed her. There wasn't anybody else in all the world – nobody but Beccs. And all she was reduced to was a few encouraging wrds ritn 2 littl on my mbile phn.

It is astonishing how quickly the publicity-pose smile

establishes itself on your face, how easy it is to get hooked on media attention. After a few days of confusion and extreme loneliness, I was hankering for my next photo-shoot for whatever magazine, my next interview for whatever paper. We all want – but some of us *need* – to feel special, I suppose. I began to feel very, very special. Chosen or destined. The things that happened just seemed to happen, as if fame and some kind of fortune were written in my stars.

I soon began to feel better about the drudgery of rehearsals, learning new songs, being taught how to dance. I thought I knew how to dance, but I didn't. There's so much you do wrong without realising it. Proper dancers made me realise it very quickly. They were so good, so fluid. I had so much to learn.

Not only about dancing – about singing, about make-up for photo-shoots, for performances, for public appearances, for television. There was so much to it. I felt as if I was at some very hurried finishing school for starlets, with mad tutors dashing me through a more bizarre but just as exacting curriculum as the national one my mum so suffered from.

Ray Ray delivered me to my new school in the huge house of Mr Jim McGregor or Mr John Fine, dashing me away from my own home and old school when things became too hot and overcrowded there. I couldn't concentrate with press-faces squashed against our downstairs windows, when the postman couldn't get through without a fight and so many friends I never knew I had kept turning up uninvited to try to see me.

When my mother read the local paper and suddenly realised that the boy who was with the one killed in the police chase was the same boy I'd been with earlier that evening, Ray Ray had been there to whisk me away. He saw the gathering clouds of stress and whipped me from there before my little sisters could think to eat any more of my eyeliner, or lipstick my dad's beige trousers any redder. How he managed to stop my mother I'll never know, but Ray had a way. Oh yes, he had a way all right.

'Poo!' he yelled at Jo and George.

They laughed. Of course they did – it was the funniest word in the world, and they had a good five or six or even seven years of believing so yet to go. 'Poo!' they shouted back.

'Poo!' while my mother tried to question me about poor Geoff and Ben and I tried to avoid her questions.

It was a long time before I found out whose place I was staying in. Jim McGregor, big Scotsman and John Fine, small Londoner both came and went whenever they liked, looking in on me with the kind of detached interest that didn't give a damn about me, except as the vehicle of their most recent songs. Neither of them ever actually spoke to me, preferring to ask the experts about my well-being, my blossoming abilities and talent. They always kept out of the way when the press were invited. I didn't work that one out till later, but I came to realise that they would have detracted from the purity of the product: me. I was supposed to be doing all this myself, as if Amy Peppercorn was an artist, a pure untainted personality in a neat little package.

The truth is, I did as I was told. The real experts told me what to do and when; I did as I was told when I was told. I had to ask permission to go back to school for the morning when Beccs called me to say that they were having a memorial assembly for Geoff. I wanted to go back anyway, to say goodbye to everybody now that school was off the agenda, now that A-level Maths was a past nightmare. I wanted to say goodbye to my teachers, to let them see how I'd be all right without them. People like me – true artists – shouldn't have to be evaluated by examination boards. We should be judged on our merits – the immense value of being such a Little Amy Peppercorn in the world.

I had to pull myself up with a start. For being such a Little Amy Peppercorn! What was I thinking? The assembly was going to be for Geoffrey Fryer, not for Amy Peppercorn! The sudden realisation of what I'd been thinking made me shudder with shame, hoping that no one had noticed me thinking like that. It would have been like picking your nose in public.

'More notice,' Ray Ray said when I told him I was going. 'Arrangements, yeah? They don't get made like that. Not just like that.'

'Arrangements?' I said.

'Arrangements,' he nodded, as if that was supposed to be an end to it.

'What arrangements? I'm just going back to school for the morning. He was a good friend of mine. He was in our band. He was in Car Crime and he –'

'School?' Ray looked around the studios, scanning the recording equipment, the masses of leads and mikes and massive headphones. 'Your dad. Talk to him. He spoke to them.'

'Yes, I know. But I'm only going back to – to say goodbye. They're holding a service for Geoffrey Fryer, before his funeral. That's another thing –'

'Right!' Ray snapped, snapping the end off the conversation. 'Right. Tomorrow. Morning only. Go in a car. Come back. Not now. Right? Right?'

No argument. Go in a car, with a driver, be taken to the school, go in, come out, come back. That's it. That was Ray. Raymond Raymond, Solar light and darkness.

He knew people, Raymond; they knew him. People came round, did as they were told. Ray was on the blower, on landline and mobile, snapping open and closed, smiling sometimes, whenever, but broadly, so that you could hear it in his voice. Ray Ray smiled, all your senses picked up on it, like the tingle you sometimes get from a piece of music. Or rather the opposite to that – an anti-tingle of foreboding as Raymond smiled into the telephone receiver at whatever, whenever.

***

Next morning, waiting to get me to school on time as if I was still a student, there was a car. There was a driver. There was no need to tell him where we were going. I got in the back, we went there.

Or, should I say, we tried to. I was in the back of the car talking to Beccs on my mobile when she said: 'I know you're coming to the assembly. The whole school knows, and everyone else, by the looks of it.'

Because the looks of it were like this as we pulled up: crowds of kids, cameras, television, policemen, with parked cars all over the place. Our car was almost immediately swallowed in the crowd. Faces pressed at the windows. Lightning flashed from cameras too near to see through. My driver looked worriedly round as thumps and claps clumped against the sides and the bonnet of the big black car.

'I'll get out!' I called to him, trying to open my door. My mobile phone line was still open to Beccs, but there was no hearing anything above the cat-calls and the shouts and screams. I couldn't get my door open.

'Stay in the car,' the driver tried to say, with a kind of urgency, near-fear in his voice.

'Stay here. Don't –'

It was good advice, I suppose. It would have prevented me being lifted, hoisted as soon as I was out by so many hands, being driven by the current of the crowd down the street away from the place I'd intended to go.

'Beccs!' I tried to shout into my mobile. I don't know if she heard me or not – I suspect not. I couldn't hear her. I couldn't hear a friend at all, only the voices of the crowd. My old life, everyone I'd ever known, everyone I'd known who'd died, was there, being remembered in that place that the crowded-out turmoil of my new life wouldn't let me reach.

Three

The specialness of being Little Amy Peppercorn was losing me in something I couldn't control. The Amy Peppercorn-ness of events would not let me honour my dead friend. If I'd ever wanted to give up things like A-level Maths, it didn't mean I wanted never to have struggled with them. I was too young to change that much that quickly, although I probably didn't really know it. But I can see little Amy P. being carried away, quite literally now. I can see and feel the excitement of the crowd combined with the anguish of not being able to make contact. It felt flattering, wonderful, exciting, scary and horrible and lonely all at once. It felt very confusing.

And as I ran away, I couldn't help feeling that I hadn't done anything yet. Not enough had been achieved to warrant such a frenzy of media attention. How could I, someone like me, be so important? And how could they have known? How could so many have known that I was going to be there?

'Come and see me at home,' I called into my mobile to Beccs, as she hung on for dear life at the other end. 'I can't get to the school. Come and see me at home.'

But, 'I can't,' she said. 'Amy, I have to go to school. It's an ordinary school day.'

I was running home. It was an ordinary day, my best friend had to remind me. Through all the crowds, through the crowded confusion, she had to remind me. She was at school, I was not.

In the background I could hear her cousin Kirsten still trying to get Beccs to hate me, saying: 'What does she want you to do? Who does she think she –'

'I've got to go,' Beccs said, cutting across the voice of Kirsty. 'They're trying to get Geoff's assembly started. Everything's all over the place. It wasn't supposed to be like this.'

I dashed home, running for cover. It wasn't supposed to be like this, not today. This was supposed to be another day, when I was famous and enjoying it.

My dad was asleep in the kitchen, with the twins rattling the bars of their cots upstairs, wailing to be set free. 'How many?' my dad said, jumping out of his sleep. 'I don't know how many,' he said blearily, as if I and not he had asked how many in the first place.

It was so good to see him. I hadn't been home for maybe two days, but it felt like twenty. It felt like two months. Running in like that, finding him blearily counting how many, with his elbow-patched cardigan and his long shorts and stained T-shirt, I could have cried.

I did cry. 'I don't know how many either,' I cried. I went to hug him.

'It's early,' he said, looking up at the kitchen clock. I looked, too. We both stood looking at it, as if the time had tricked us. 'I wasn't expecting you until –'

'You were expecting me?' I said.

'Yes. But not yet. Shouldn't you be –'

But I was looking at him in surprise. He glanced again at the clock, as if to make sure that he really wasn't expecting me.

There was a ring, then almost immediately a knock at the

door. The knock was so firm, so loud you could hear it above the furious racket Jo and George were creating upstairs. 'That'll be the door,' my dad said.

'How come you were expecting me, Dad? I didn't –'

'Let me get the door.'

'Leave it. It's only some of the people following me from school.'

'I'll get rid of them,' he said, going out.

I waited, listening to the door opening, to the conversations almost drowned out by the twins, to the silencing of my sisters when my dad brought them in, one on each arm, and they saw me and started up again as if I was something horrible that had suddenly happened.

'They're pleased to see you,' my dad said, or rather shouted.

'Yes!' I yelled back, kissing the girls.

'Hang on!' he cried; but whether he was talking to me or to them, I never knew. 'Hang on!' and he was gripping each of them by an ankle, lowering them gently until they were upside down, each suspended by a left or right leg. Instant silence. 'They love this,' he said.

The girls, fascinated by the world turned upside down, watched me wipe away the tears that were still crawling up my face.

'Now,' my dad strained, going red, 'the only – problem – is – I can't – keep this up – for long.'

I laughed.

'You – all right – Amy?' he said. 'Hang on. – Come in – the other –' he gasped, leading me into the other room, our little living room.

He launched the laughing girls on to the settee. They immediately scrambled up an arm each, setting up a trampolining competition.

'How are you, my Little Amy?' my dad said, fighting the

girls on to the floor. 'I think I'm sometimes losing a fighting battle,' he said, fighting, losing.

'And me,' I said, because he'd said what he'd said and made it too easy for me to say the same.

'You?' he said, fixing a twin on to each slipper. 'You? You've only just started, haven't you? It's all excitement, surely?'

'Yes, it is. It is, Dad, but – I don't know. It's not something – I don't feel right.'

'You don't feel right? I haven't felt right for years. I've made a virtue out of being in the wrong, I have. You'll get used to it. It's called growing up.'

'Is it? It that what it is?' There was another loud rap on the window, on the door, another ring, another window rap.

'They'll go away,' my dad said. But as he said it, I could see he hoped they wouldn't.

'I just wanted to go back to school this morning,' I said. 'I wanted to say goodbye. I wanted to say goodbye, that's all. I'm moving on without – they're making me move too fast, Dad. I can't feel anybody. Nobody's with me.'

My dad stomped over towards me, a baby sister on each foot. 'That's not true, Amy. We're with you. Your mum and me. We're with you every step of the way. Come here,' he said, taking me in his arms.

I closed my eyes. For a moment I thought I could feel the power, the strength of my mother through my dad's strong arm. Then I thought I could smell her, for a moment. Dad held me with one hand, while the other pinched one corner of a letter, holding it in the air next to my face, waiting for me to emerge tearless from his shoulder. 'This came for you this morning,' he said.

'What is it?' I said, as if he should know.

'You'd better open it,' he said, as if he *did* know.

I opened it. It was from some company I'd never heard of. 'It's – ten thousand pounds,' I stammered.

He knew. 'It's an advance on your royalties,' he shouted, picking Jo and George from the floor at his feet, 'in case you have some expenses to pay,' he bellowed, making for the door. 'Shall I make some tea?'

They left me standing in our living room, our old living room with the Teletubbies telly and the old table where my mother sat with her red marking pen every evening. A ten thousand-pound cheque made out to me, Ms A. Peppercorn, as if I were really a Ms and not so little. An amount I wasn't expecting from a company I'd never heard of.

'They're your accountants,' my dad told me in the kitchen, as the electric kettle bumped to the boil. One of the girls was being kind enough to assist the other to clamber into the tumble dryer.

'My accountants?'

'Well, they're the Solar Records accountants, so I suppose they're yours as well. That's spending money, by the way.'

'Spending money?'

'Yes. That's just an advance. The accountants will be taking care of your finances. Tax, that sort of thing. I don't even know if you'd pay tax, would you?'

'I don't know, Dad. You worked in finance, didn't you?'

'Not that sort of finance, I didn't. Anyway, the money's yours, to do what you want with.'

The money was mine. The accountants were taking care. Ray Ray was being extra careful, arranging cars, arranging nobody knew what else. My dad had been expecting me. The media, the police, a huge crowd and the press had been awaiting my arrival outside my old school.

Raymond Raymond.

I could feel his grin, the solar power of his smile as I held up a ten thousand-pound cheque with Ms A. Peppercorn on it, as plain as any solar-eclipsed day.

Four

Text to Beccs:

'WLL CLL U 2NITE. LOVE.'

Text to Ben:

'I HOPE YOU ARE RECEIVING MY MESSAGES. I'M THINKING OF YOU. GEOFF WOULDN'T BLAME YOU. GOODNIGHT, BEN.'

***

'I don't think I can, Beccs. I don't think I can do it,' with my mobile lighting up the tented space under my blankets.

It wasn't late in Jim McGregor or John Fine's fine house, but it was dark and I was tired and I wanted to be alone with my mobile under the quilt, talking to my best friend. She, at least, was there for me, hanging on the line.

'Why not?' she said. 'What's wrong with singing *If Ever* now?'

'Because it's – they'll want – you know.'

'What? They'll want a repeat performance, is that it?'

'Yes,' I said. 'That's it. And I don't know if I can. No, I don't know if I *should*. I gave that to Geoff. If I do it again, it'll be for other reasons. I'll be more like what Kirsty thinks of me.'

And then I'd said the wrong thing. I could tell by the tented telephone silence that Beccs didn't like me referring to her cousin like that. I didn't like it either. It sounded as if I was trying to draw Beccs into siding with me. I wasn't doing that, honestly. I'm not like that. 'I mean,' I said, 'that it'll be as if I'm using Geoff. Beccs, I wouldn't do that.'

She had already told me what had happened at the memorial assembly at school. She said that the commotion had turned it into a farce, with no one really listening to the service or to what was being said. 'They wanted to know about you,' Beccs told me. 'They wanted information about you.'

'What did you tell them?' I asked.

'I didn't tell them anything,' she said, but added 'I didn't' as if somebody else had. I thought I could guess who had been talking about me but I managed, that time, not to say anything.

Almost every other thing we had to say to each other, I had to watch what I was saying. Every second sentence from me sounded like some kind of boast, or a dig at somebody (usually Kirsty), or an attempt to get Beccs to side with me. I didn't want there to be any sides.

'I'm doing a chat show tomorrow,' I told her.

'Which one?' she said.

'That one with Frank Fisher, you know?'

'Frank Fisher?' Beccs said. 'I like him. He's funny.'

'Yeah,' I said. 'But they want me to do *If Ever*. I'm supposed to come on and sing it before he talks to me.'

'Are you?' Beccs said, as if what I'd just said was boasting rather than an expression of my reluctance to do that song on TV, or anywhere, ever again.

I told her I couldn't bring on the tears just because of the cameras. I said I hadn't done it for that. She said she knew. I really hoped she'd remember that, so that no cousins or any other kind of relative could possibly convince her otherwise.

'I think you should,' she said.

'You do?' I said. 'You think I should just sing it again?'

'Yes,' she said, stopping there as if a simple yes or no was all there was to it. The phone line was awfully, conspicuously silent. I thought, for one terrible moment, I could feel Ray Ray grinning over Beccs's shoulder at the opposite end of the line.

'I'm not sure I can,' I said.

'Don't worry about it,' she said. 'It's okay. I know how you feel, but Geoff wouldn't want you not to sing it, would he?'

'I don't know. Wouldn't he?'

'Of course he wouldn't. Of all of us, he was the only one really pleased for you when we all found out about Solar.'

'Was he? He didn't – I didn't –'

'No, well . . . He was too worried about other things. Believe me, he was pleased for you. He was the only one who wasn't jealous. If you're thinking about Geoff, that's a reason to go on and sing it, not a reason not to.'

Beccs. I loved her. My best friend. I was aching, dying to see her. People were with me, round me, *at* me all day, and I was lonelier than I'd ever been in my life.

'Beccs,' I said, 'don't go away, will you? Don't ever go away.'

'I won't,' she said. 'I'm here. I'm right here.'

And for a moment here was here, where I was, wherever that might be. I needed a friend desperately, absolutely.

'I'm sorry about today,' I said. 'It shouldn't have been like that. It shouldn't have been like that at all.'

'No,' she said. 'But it wasn't your fault. You're not to blame for everything, Amy. Geoff's mum was there. She was fine. She understood.'

'Did she? How do you know?'

'I was with her most of the time. Nobody knew she was

coming. She was lovely. She wasn't crying. She wasn't blaming anyone – not Ben, not anyone. She's lovely. The newspapers were asking her lots of questions –'

'Were they?'

'She's fine though. "They're bound to ask," she said to me, about the papers. All she did say was to ask me if I could ask you – she doesn't want any fuss at Geoff's funeral tomorrow. She asked me to ask you if you wouldn't mind – if all of us could stay away tomorrow.'

'Oh,' I said. 'Oh.'

'That's what she said. I said that's fine. I didn't think you'd be able to go anyway. You wouldn't, would you, what with the show and everything?'

'No,' I said. 'No, you're right.'

'No. That's what I thought. I said we wouldn't be there, if that's what she wanted. That's what she wanted, she said. Except for Kirsty. She wanted Kirsty to go, because of Geoff. Because Geoff was – because Kirsty was special to Geoff, Mrs Fryer wants her to go.'

'Does she?'

'Only I don't think Kirsty wants to go, because she hates funerals. And nobody should go to a funeral if they don't want to, should they?'

'No,' I said. 'No. Nobody should.'

***

If Ever was at the top of the charts for the third week. Courtney Schaeffer's latest had peaked at twelve or thereabouts, and was on its way back down. I read in yesterday's papers that she was going to be twenty next week. No longer a teenager. The paper made her sound old. They made it sound as if they were bored with her.

Ray Ray was always bellowing over my shoulder, shuddering through the open pages of all the old newspapers flung around in Jim McGregor or John Fine's house. The two dried songsmiths were forever locking themselves away, appearing for fresh coffee, a change of newspaper. They saw me reading sometimes, but hardly noticed me. Raymond would come to me with their songs, accompanied by my accompanist, my piano player Leo. Lovely Leo had to give me the tunes I couldn't read to go with the ordinary words I could.

'Lovely, Sweet,' Leo would smack, nodding his curly head.

Yesterday's papers were all I could find this morning. John Fine had been briefly spotted earlier in the morning with his arms full, disappearing into the smoky composition den, the lyric lair from where the two pieced together tunes with ordinary words. Ray Ray was barking into Leo's sensitive face. Janie, my choreographer and dance tutor, wasn't here for once. All week she'd been grinding my legs ever shorter in the studios. I was doing *If Ever* tonight on Frank Fisher, so no dancing included. No tears either, I'd promised myself. This time it was going to be different.

'All set?' Ray came clattering, coffee pots, cups, a plate of toast. He ate as he spoke, very quickly, very loudly. He slurped strong black coffee, masses of sugar stirred in. 'Frank Fisher? Very funny. Do us good, yeah?'

'Yeah?' I said.

Lovely Leo was tinkling at the keyboard of the baby grand piano in the next room. But it wasn't a separate room – it was just the next bit of the house, the bit round the next corner. Ray was standing in the big kitchen bit, I was sitting at one of the black shiny breakfast bars with yesterday's paper. Courtney Schaeffer was on her way back down the charts. We were still on top:

Number One: *If Ever* – Little Amy Peppercorn

Number Eight: *The Word On The Street* – Little Amy Peppercorn

Number Twelve-ish: *Something or the Other* – Courtney Schaeffer

'Yeah,' Ray sputtered, his toast generously shared with worktop and big blowsy kettle. 'Yeah. Frank Fisher? Top man. Listen. You all right, are you?'

'Yes,' I said. 'Yes, I think so.'

Leo purred up and down the major and minor keys from round the corner, where the next bit of the house housed the baby grand on polished blond floorboards, one or two elegant sculptures, very little else. This house was a minimalist heaven that exposed you in its vast open spaces, its sparsity of furniture, televisions or gadgets. I had to go to my bedroom to watch TV or listen to music, other than Leo's lovely embellishments on the piano. Perhaps the great songwriters were made more comfortable in their lyric lair but I don't know, because I was never allowed in there.

'Your mum and dad,' Ray said. He stuffed a good two-thirds of a piece of heavily buttered toast into his fast face, grinding everything to crumbs. 'Tonight,'– champ, champ. 'All right?'

'Yes,' I said, understanding Ray Ray as simply as his simplicity of speech. Tonight, all right, my parents were going to be there, in the audience. My second TV appearance, my parents would have witnessed both. I was pleased, I suppose, although I didn't altogether feel it.

'You right for it?' Ray champed. He ate as if he was biting great lumps out of the world, to make them wholly his and never anybody else's. He, almost more than the songwriters themselves, had the run of the Fine Mansion and all its facilities.

'I'm fine,' I said, beginning to feel unnerved that Ray was showing too much concern.

'Sure?' he smiled, like a crocodile.

'I'm fine,' I said again.

'Parents there,' he said. 'All emotions intact. Should be right for it.'

I knew what it was, in actual fact. Ray wanted tears from me. He wanted a repeat performance for me to turn on the taps for the television cameras. He wanted to see the evidence of salt water sparkling in my eyes permanently to keep me just this side, and only just this side, of tears. 'I'm fine,' I said.

Leo was tinkling up and down in the next space, filling up the open distances everywhere with tuneless scales. Ray was concentrating on me. Leo was waiting, doing the piano-player's equivalent of drumming his fingers.

'That song,' Ray said. '*If Ever.* It needs, you know? Emotional – spark? Yeah?'

'I know what that song needs,' I said.

Leo drummed, tinkling louder than before, growing impatient.

'Good,' Ray champed. 'Good.'

'I can sing it,' I said. 'Don't worry.'

'No,' he said, through Leo's impatience. 'No. Not only that.'

'I'll sing it,' I said.

'Not only that, though,' he insisted, his last piece of toast discarded, half eaten, broken into little bits.

'I'm a singer,' I said.

'Performer –' looking, glancing towards where Leo could be heard but not seen.

'Whatever.'

'Not whatever.'

'Yeah, whatever.'

***

Text:

'BEN. CAN I WRITE YOU? LOVE. AMY.'

Text:

'BEN. CLL ME B4 SHOW 2NITE. AMY.'

'Take no notice, Sweet,' Leo was saying to me. 'You're lovely, he's not. He's an ogre, an absolute ogre. Now, why don't we see what we can do with some of this McGregor and Fine tat, shall we?' Leo's hand went to his mouth and he turned, giggling, on his piano seat, towards the M and F den.

I laughed. Leo always managed to make me laugh. I loved the way he had of making me feel that I'd always known him, that we'd always been friends and always would be. Leo had a lovely way of making me feel I'd never need to be texting him all day on a Saturday, trying to get through to the voice of a friend. Leo was just there, giggling on a piano stool as if I'd giggled with him ever since we were both little.

'No,' he said, 'no, really, Sweet, they're so lucky to have found you. That voice of yours. Lovely, so very lovely. One day, Darling, you'll have those two old smoky misters and that ogre at your feet. Believe me, that day is coming.'

The stink of cigar and cigarette billowed from the composers' smoking den, filling an otherwise non-smoking house. Leo loved it, practically falling to the ground giggling behind his hand as I rushed from the kitchen to the smoking den with a domestic fire extinguisher. 'How can they breathe in there?' I laughed.

We had to run away quickly, arranging ourselves at Leo's piano as one of the M and F team came to the open door after us. Big Jim McG. stood for a moment, florid face chomping on a fat cigar, loose-leafed paper in his huge hand. He stood at the door of the den for a few moments, watching us from afar as Leo's fluid fingers ran the length of the piano keyboard.

'Ready, Lovely?' he sang, because I couldn't with laughing so much. 'Let's have another go at this one. It's our favourite,' he said, looking past me to Jim McGregor, who disappeared behind the den door with a half-shake of his head.

We laughed, Lovely Leo and me, for just about the whole day. He was with me, breakfast, lunch, early light dinner, getting me ready for the Frank Fisher Show that night. Frank Fisher was on quite late, so there wasn't any real hurry. I couldn't get through to Beccs on her mobile and didn't want to call her home and speak to her mother – I don't know why. I couldn't get through to Ben. I didn't want to speak to his mother, knowing only too well why. I called my mum and my dad answered. Mum was in the shower. The twins were unwell, he thought. They were red-cheeked and roaring with coughs and bad colds. 'Get Mum to call my mobile when she gets out,' I had to yell as he disappeared from the line.

My mum didn't have a mobile. She hated them. My dad pretended to like his, but the battery was always run down.

Beccs's mobile was run down too, by the sound of it. 'Please leave me a message,' it said, 'or I'll never call you back.' Which was exactly the same as Ben's before it went dead.

I never knew what Geoff's message sounded like before it went – before it became unobtainable. Because that's what Geoff was now, even more than Ben: unobtainable. The mobile lines travelled through the air like – maybe – Geoff, but he wasn't there. Geoff wasn't obtainable by land or air. He'd been cremated this afternoon.

Yesterday, I'd been dancing pretty well all day. Janie, my dance tutor, was a ton of bricks on me, bearing down on my little legs all day while Leo played piano. Janie was, had been, a brilliant and beautiful dancer. Now she limped in with her walking stick, still surprisingly young, still looking fit, but with her joints wasting away too quickly inside her. She worked me until I could barely stand, her serious face disapproving of just about everything I tried to do.

I did try. I tried and tried. I felt like crying, trying not to think of Geoff's funeral. I tried and tried not to think of Geoff's funeral, but the air somewhere must have been thick with poor Geoffrey's passing as the smoke that blanketed under the door of the den in the Fine Mansion.

Last night, I'd texted Beccs:

'GF – RIP.'

She wasn't available; I think I understand why. She didn't want to talk to anybody. Neither did I, really. Except Beccs. But I understood if she wanted to speak to nobody at all.

'GF – RIP.'

Five

In the car on the way to the television studios, I tried Beccs's mobile again. Again Ben's message came back at me in Beccs's voice. If I didn't leave her a message, she'd never call me back. Well, I had left her messages, several of them, none of which had produced a response. I called home. Our phone rang and rang, then went into a standard message reply: 'The person you have called is not available at the moment.'

It sounded so impersonal. Our home number never used to say that – it used to be me speaking, as I was then, not erased as I am now.

I called Beccs at home. I didn't want to – I don't know why.

'Hello, Amy,' her mother said. 'How are you?'

'I'm fine, thanks, Mrs Bradley. Is Rebecca there?'

'No, I'm afraid she isn't. She's gone to Kirsty's, to watch you on the – what is it you're on tonight?'

'Frank Fisher.'

'Yes. She'll be sleeping over. Why don't you call her there?'

That, then, was why I hadn't wanted to call her at home. I knew she might not be there. I knew she could be – she'd be where she was when I most needed to speak to her and her alone.

I had to call Kirsty's house and speak to her mum. 'Who's calling?'

'Amy.'

'Amy . . . Oh, Amy? Hello. You're causing quite a little stir at the moment, aren't you?'

I had to say yes, I supposed I was, although I didn't quite understand what she meant. From Kirsten's mother it sounded barbed – a bit like an accusation, a bit like an insult. 'Is Beccs there, Mrs McCloud, please?'

'No,' she said, still with a note of accusation in her voice. 'I'm sorry, she isn't. I'm not expecting them back till quite late tonight, after that poor boy's funeral. They'll be back in time to – oh, yes, that's right; they'll be back to see you on that talk show tonight. That's why you didn't go to the funeral, I suppose, is it?'

'Yes,' I said. 'That's it.'

'Still,' she said, 'it must be very difficult for you, just finding time for everything. Keeping in touch with your friends must be very difficult.'

'Yes,' I said. 'Yes, it is.'

Yes. Yes, it was. My friends were becoming unobtainable, some permanently. Mobiles were switched off for the funeral none of us were supposed to be attending, according to my best friend. Mrs Fryer hadn't wanted us there, Beccs said. Now I could see it was me – only me she didn't want there. Or me and Ben. Well, I don't suppose she wanted Geoff to have to be there, really. But only I was asked not to attend. Only I caused a troublesome commotion wherever I went.

I created situations that forced Beccs to lie to me. I didn't mean to – situations just happened round me, completely out of my control. Car Crime seemed to just smash in my face again and again, like the fragmented windscreen that Geoff must have flown into.

The early London lights flickered across the standby face of my mobile phone, which remained resolutely unlit with no messages coming in. Nobody told me the truth, or bothered to explain anything.

My dressing room, when I got there, had my name on it in what looked like some kind of permanent lettering. The receptionist had been expecting me. She was, indeed, very anxious to meet me. She liked my song, she told me, looking at me as I signed in.

'You must get to meet all sorts of people,' I said, handing her back her very expensive-looking pen.

'Oh, yes,' she said, 'but they're not very nice, a lot of them. A lot of them think they're God's gift. They treat you like dirt, a lot of them. Anyway, I don't suppose you've got to that stage yet.'

'I never will,' I assured her.

She smiled, unassured. 'Well, anyway,' she said, 'Harry will take you to your dressing room.'

'Thank you,' I said, trying to smile at the security guard in his uniform.

Through what seemed like about half a kilometre of corridor, stern-faced Harry, guarding my security, wasn't going to be treated like dirt by anyone, his silence told me. He delivered me to my own, my very own dressing room. He nodded once at my thank you, striding away down the corridor with keys clinking in his big secure pockets.

I opened the door. Inside, my dressing room was huge, with a sink and a little two-piece suite and a writing table with flowers and a chair for the table and another in front of the lighted mirror. A peppercorn assault of various newspapers and magazines slewed across the table.

If Beccs had been available, obtainable, I'd have called her to tell her about it. I wanted to be able to tell her everything as it happened, to share it with her. I wanted her to be a part of everything that happened to me, as if it was happening to her too.

But Beccs was with Kirsty after the funeral, not here with me. I was here on my own, supposed to be having a good time, flying high, loving it. I was supposed to be living the dream. This should have been it. There were flowers on my very own dressing table, there was a painted nameplate on the door. There were newspapers and style mags with my smiling or crying mugshot caught in the flashing electronic limelight.

They made me look so much older, so much more in or out of control. I could see the artifice, the trick of everything that was supposedly done in my name or on my behalf. It all looked as if I was in control of everything but my emotions, as if I was steering all this poster publicity and excitement. Kirsty's mum had seemed to accuse me of creating a furore in a frenzied attempt to publicize myself. She was wrong, so very wrong. All I had to do was walk over to the table and pick up today's newspaper to see how very wrong she was:

'NEW STAR IN SCHOOL DEATH DRAMA!'

How very wrong. How very, very wrong.

A huge headline emblazoned above another face, supposedly my own, caught startled in the headlines like a rabbit in the headlights of a rapidly approaching car.

New singing sensation Little Amy Peppercorn was in the middle of an intrigue, attending the funeral service of a friend allegedly killed by the reckless and illegal driving of another youth. The illegal driver, who is an unlicensed 17-year-old, is reported to be a very special friend of Ms Peppercorn. The young offender is being held in custody, although he is currently hospitalised and recovering from injuries sustained as a result of the car crash.

The relationship between the up-and-coming young singing star and the joyrider is said to be close, centred around a dance band calling itself Car Crime.

Then another picture of my startled face appearing from the back of another car into the bully crowd of Geoff's ruined memorial assembly the other day. Then, somehow, a picture of a bent and buckled car, with the legend 'Car Crime' in black, funereal letters thickened underneath. Car Crime the headline, Car Crime the caption to the photo showing another motor entirely. This was not the one I'd seen Ben in. This was either his second steal of the evening or it was an impostor, a newspaper set-up of another crime in which Geoff Fryer might have died but didn't.

This car crime, that Amy Peppercorn – both were impostors dreamed up by newspapers whose stories made intimate my relationship with Ben as he waited to be taken from hospital and put on remand.

Car Crime was in all the newspapers – my name and Geoff's, no Beccs or Kirsten, with Ben hinted at, referred to as another youth (17), the alleged joyrider, man-slaughterer, killer. Geoff's killer, with me as his accomplice. The new singing sensation, killer's accomplice, in school death drama.

School death dramas were reported on in this way, read out of morbid curiosity by everyone unfeeling for the death of a youth (16). Sixteen! Then Geoff's parents, his loving mother, will have had to see, to read, to feel the report of the death of the sixteen-year-old son that I'd managed to publicise so effectively. I was the only one, in the event, not allowed to attend the funeral today – the only one creating all this excitement, this furore.

There were no pictures of Geoff. My tears had to fall on to my own startled face, placking against my own eyes, running blackened newsprint down my face like watered mascara. Or I blinked against the bogus car crime, the broken car they'd pictured to try to make the killing more satisfying for an inquisitive public, making it more juicy, more close to being bloody. I had to cry on my own against the false broken images, against the terminal telephone messages, unobtainable friends and family. All I had was a knock on the door, a rapping that couldn't be a friend of mine.

The newspapers and the shiny magazines slipped on to the floor. One more knock and the door opened without a word from me.

Two words came through: 'Make-up!' in a woman's voice.

'Yes,' I sniffed, wiping my eyes. 'Yes. Make-up.'

The make-up artist came flinging in, telling me her name was June – as sunny as June itself, as she said herself. I wouldn't have said it. I couldn't say anything, blinking back my tears, wiping the newsprint from my fingers on to my face.

'Never mind,' June said, bustling me into a chair. 'It doesn't matter. Let's have a go with some of this,' she said, prising back my head, slapping me in the saddened face with a plentiful palm full of simple cleansing cream.

So June the make-up queen made up my face as she went along, inventing for me an attitude, a television picture image to hide the newspaper imprint of my tears. So easily did she cover me with her TV trickery, that when Ray Ray burst from behind my cloud I too shone like a secondary sun in, and under, June.

'Everything all right?' he came and said and went and then came back. 'Sure? Everything?'

I nodded, trying not to smudge June all over my face. I tried not to think of Geoff's mum trying not to think of what it feels like when cars crash. I tried not to think of what it feels like afterwards for all those left behind.

'You ready?' Raymond Raymond asked again and again. I nodded that I was, giving nothing away – not to him.

'Good!' he yapped. 'Good!' And glanced at the papers in a pyre under the memorial of flowers on the table.

'Good! Ready! Good!'

June brushed tears into my eyes, still making me up as she went along. I went along with it, pretending to be ready for this. I was pretending that it didn't matter that Ray had set me up. He'd kept me from today's news until tonight, until it suited his purpose to unleash the latest stories on me. I had to pretend I didn't care what he was doing to me, how he was engineering my emotions for his not-so-hidden agenda.

I was going to sing the song I'd sung to my friend, but now Ray Ray knew it was for Geoff – as, I supposed, looking at the papers, did everyone else. Now Ray wanted to keep me pumped full of tears, primed with all the right emotions he could tap at will.

But my salt water was turning bitter, running back down the tubes to sour my mouth. Nobody knew or could understand the sort of pressure I was under.

On this side of the magazine and television camera, this side of the truth, the walk to the stage trod heavy with responsibility. Raymond walked with me, rubbing my face in it. 'Your mum. She couldn't make it. Something about Jo or George. Not very well.'

'Oh,' I said, with his hand on my shoulder in an authoritative grip rather than any kind of friendly or reassuring touch.

'Dad's here, though,' he said, guiding me into position on a little stage with dark blue drapes and more dying flowers.

I had to wait there for my signal to start singing. When

they said, whenever they said, indicating with little red lights and clipboard girls' nods on cue, I was to turn it on like a tap, watering the world of easy entertainment and cut funereal flowers.

On cue, the indicators blinked, the clipboards clicked and the curtains opened to give me up to the audience. As preordained, I started singing when I was supposed to start, stopping exactly on time. In between, my voice soared as the audience and my proud dad stared with tears in their and his eyes, and an empty seat by my dad's side.

You could seize the day for me
Keep the night away for me
Make the darkness light for me
The noble sun ignite for me,
If ever, if ever you were here.

I sang for Geoff.

No, not for Geoff. Not for him, although I tried. I tried and tried to give the song to him.

And if ever you were here again
I'd never shed a tear again
Or make the sunrise mine alone
Or see a new sun shine alone,
If ever, if ever you were here.

No matter how hard I tried to give the song away, to make it, to keep it Geoff's, it came right back to me.

If ever you were here with me
Once more . . .

I wanted to look for Geoff but could find only myself in a flood of tears and an empty chair by my dad's left-leaning elbow.

Just one more day to keep
As darkness makes its way to sleep . . .

And nothing left of me to offer the nothing now left of Geoff but tears shed for myself, for me alone, with no one else to understand what I was going through.

To know that you've been near again
I'd never, ever shed a tear again.

For me, selfishly, shamefully.

For the last and final time. I would not be doing this again. This was it, my second and final public performance of *If Ever*. I'd never, ever shed a tear again.

***

Frank Fisher gave me a box of tissues as the applause rang in my ears like a shell. I had to go from the stage to talk to him, sitting on a settee with him in an armchair. The tissues had been sitting on a little table by his chair waiting expectantly for me, like a prop for a joke. Frank Fisher was a comedian, waiting for the hollow clapping to start to abate before handing me the tissues, turning applause to laughter at his say-so. He was a master at controlling his audience, as much as I felt a victim of mine. So when his audience and mine were one and the same, he could victimise me through them at will, as easily as handing me a whole box of very elaborate tissues, kissing me on both cheeks. I could smell the cigarettes on his breath.

'Welcome to the show,' he said. I think I nodded, I'm not sure. My mum taped the show, but I've never been able to bring myself to watch it. 'Do you want to blow your nose or something?' he said as I dabbed my eyes.

'No, I'm fine,' I managed to say.

'That's some fantastically emotional performance,' he said. 'Tell me, how do you manage to – you know, turn it on like that? I mean, you look as if someone's nicked your lottery ticket.' Some laughter came, not much. 'Or your boyfriend.' More laughter. Frank Fisher was sitting smiling at me as if he knew something. He did. Everyone did.

'No,' he said, 'really, that's some performance, isn't it, ladies and gentlemen?' He turned to his audience as they victimised me again with their empty applause.

'Little Amy Peppercorn, eh?' Frank Fisher said, smiling at me again. 'So, how tall are you, Amy, actually?'

'Oh,' I said, trotting out my old line, 'I'd be a good two metres.'

'Really?' he said as the audience rippled. He took me by the hand, stood me up next to him. 'I never knew I was so tall,' he said. 'Crikey, I must be a bit of a giant.'

He let me sit down. At least the audience appreciated it. I didn't.

'No, listen,' he said, as if I wasn't, 'you've done brilliantly. A Number One hit, with another song flying up the charts. What's it called, the other one?'

'*The Word on the Street.*'

'Yeah. Good song, too. How do you – tell me – how do you – I mean, is it luck? Two records, just like that? I understand you're still at school?'

'No, not now. I was, doing my A-levels.'

'But I suppose, what with your success and everything, school's out for summer, and winter too, is it?'

'Well, for the moment. I can always take A-levels in the future.'

'Yeah, but I bet you're hoping you don't have to, aren't you? You're in the entertainment business now. That'll learn you all the lessons you'll ever need to know, take my word for it.'

'I will,' I said, looking at him. Something in Frank's dishonest smile told me how much he didn't like me. Something in the way he was looking back at me said that overnight successes like mine, kids like me finding success with his hard-won audience, left a taste in his mouth more dry and bitter than the after-flavour of his filter-tipped cigarettes.

'No, listen,' he said again, 'good luck with it, really. The emotion in it when you do that – how do you do that? I mean, how do you – you know, tears, big emotions? Fantastic, really. But how do you do it?'

'I don't know,' I said. 'I don't think I – it's really not something I –'

'Lots of stuff about you in the papers this morning. Boyfriend in jail, isn't it? Another mate killed in a car. Plenty to cry about, I suppose. Is it true? Your boyfriend?'

'No.'

'No?'

'No.'

'Oh. It's not true. All that stuff in the newspapers. None of it?'

I breathed, blinked. I didn't want to do this. Any of it. 'I don't want to – it's not anybody's business, that's all.'

'Isn't it?' he said, with a comedian's look of blank innocence. 'When it's all over the newspapers? You're in the entertainment business now, you know. It's everyone's business. That's entertainment. It's a hard lesson.'

'Yes,' I said.

'Yes,' he said. 'Anyway, Courtney Schaeffer. What about her then, eh? She's been giving you some stick in the press too, hasn't she?'

'Has she?'

'Just a bit. I read . . . hang on,' he said, reaching behind his chair for one of today's papers. 'Listen here: "Amy Peppercorn's just a mini-me. She's trying to do everything I do, only in miniature." That's her. Didn't you see it?'

'No.'

'Sounds a bit miffed, doesn't she?'

'A bit.'

'Do you care?'

'No. Why should I? I don't care what she says about me. I'm sure she doesn't care what I say about her. She can't sing as well as I can, I know that much. She knows it too, but I'm sure she'll say she doesn't care what I say. If you like her, you like her.'

'Do you like her?'

'I – don't – she's not my – no, I don't – she doesn't do what I like.'

'I don't think she's all that keen on you either.' The audience, for some reason, wanted to find that funny.

It's funny, but when you're up there or down there, under intense scrutiny like that, being interviewed by someone with another hidden, hostile agenda, the funny things that people want to laugh at aren't funny in the least. People like Frank Fisher smell of cigarette smoke and exude an anti-charm of antagonism that is not funny in the least.

'Courtney thinks that the crying's a cute trick on your part. She says that once the crying stops, it's goodbye Little Amy Peppercorn.'

I couldn't stop looking at Frank's lower jaw, the way his teeth ground as he smiled, the way his camera-camaraderie gnashed at me in a crush of dead spit and nicotine.

'The tears *have* stopped,' I said.

'Really?' he said, smiling at his audience. 'The tears have stopped?'

'Yes. That was – they were the last. I'm not doing it any more.'

'What, crying?'

'That's right. It's finished. So we'll see what Courtney Schaeffer has to say about that. That was my last public performance of *If Ever.*'

Frank looked at his audience again. 'That was – *is* your Number One hit, and that was the last time you're ever going to sing it? Is that what you're saying?'

'That's exactly what I'm saying. I'm not doing it any more. It's too personal.'

'Blimey!' he exclaimed, turning away from me. 'Ladies and gentlemen,' he said, holding out his arms, 'you heard it here first. Or rather you heard it here last. The last performance of *If Ever*, on the Frank Fisher Show. Amy Peppercorn, Little Amy, it's been wonderful having you on the show.'

And Frank Fisher shook my hand as the audience warmly applauded, with Frank looking down into my face as if he'd done something spiteful and got away with it. He looked very, very pleased, anyway.

***

'Who do you! You think you can! I've a good mind to! If you weren't!'

Ray Ray had exploded, jumping unexpectedly into the front of the car with my dad as he started the engine for the journey home. Ray couldn't finish a single sentence. Everything he said, or tried to say, was spat from between clenched front teeth, his red face seething, his invective stopping him short every time. He couldn't breathe properly, he was so purple-angry.

My dad, doing the driving, kept nodding at Ray, then

glancing at me in the rear-view mirror. 'Amy –' he'd start to say.

'If she wasn't!' Ray would spit, grinding his teeth. 'I've a good mind!'

I almost laughed at that one. 'I'm just not doing it again,' I said again, for about the sixteenth time.

'You!' Ray raged, his reddening face appearing to darken between the passing streetlamps. 'Who do you!'

'Amy –' my dad attempted again.

'Who does she!' Ray turned to him, barking in his face. 'It's not for her to!'

'It's not for you to say,' my dad turned to say.

'Who does she think she!' Ray barked.

'You can't go doing things like that,' my dad said, through the reflection in the rear-view.

'Well, I've done it. That's it. It's done.' And I felt so much better about it. Especially having done it, made the public announcement in the way I did. It gave Raymond Raymond no opportunity to prevent it or reverse my decision. 'What's done's done,' I said.

All we could hear was the sound of Ray's teeth cracking for the rest of the journey home. All I could sense was the disapproval of my dad reflected back on me when he should have been worrying about his driving. But all I could feel was the relief of not having to exploit Geoffrey Fryer's death again, or Ben's incarceration. The second time of singing *If Ever* in public was one too many; any more were out of the question. Little Amy wasn't having anything to do with it, whatever the damage to my mad, maddeningly brief career, or the cost to Solar Records or Ray Ray. Especially Ray: the more angry he became the more convinced I was that I had made the right decision.

My mum leapt awake from the settee as we came in in full

thump and red Raymond's blaze of fury. 'Of all the!' he started, throwing a new tantrum for the sake of my bleary mum. 'Did you see?'

My mum nodded, glancing at my dad.

'I've a good mind!' Ray raged.

'No!' my mum said, deciding, as I had, against Ray's good mind. 'Keep your voices down! The girls are asleep,' she announced, trouncing Ray's rage without once looking at him or at me. She was looking straight at my dad as if he'd been the one shouting the odds up the garden path and in through the front door.

'Did you see the show?' my dad said quietly, with everything brought back down to earth.

'Some of it,' my mum said. The show didn't sound at all important when she talked about it.

Ray stood in the shadows of the low lamp stand, his face shrouded, his self-importance battered by my mum's lack of concern.

'Shall I make a cup of tea?' I asked.

'I'll have one,' my dad said.

My mum shook her head. 'I've got to go to bed. I'm very tired.' And she looked very, very tired. But she didn't move, standing there on the other side of the low lamp, keeping the wrath of Solar Records at bay as Ray seethed powerlessly out of the light.

'Ray?' I said.

'Got to go,' he rumbled. 'All sorts of sorting to do.'

'Okay,' I said. But we still didn't move, any of us.

'Early, in the morning,' Ray said.

'Okay,' I said again. Tomorrow was Sunday. It didn't make any difference.

He turned, went out, closing the front door gently behind him. I smiled. He'd forgotten that he'd come back with us, ranting and raving in my dad's car. That meant he'd be walking down our garden path into the street before realising he didn't have any transport.

'I'll make a cup of tea, then,' I said, 'shall I?'

Ray didn't come back. I knew he wouldn't.

'You shouldn't have done that, Amy,' my dad said. 'Why did you do it?'

'She has her reasons,' my mum said.

'I know she has her reasons,' he said. 'I just wanted to know what they were.'

'She has her own reasons,' she said again.

I felt like thanking her, hugging her, giving her my reasons. I would have done all those things if she hadn't stopped me, denying my gratitude by saying: 'Her reasons are nothing to do with you, Tony. Or me. Just go and make some tea, Amy, if you're going.'

'But surely –' my dad started to say.

'Look, what difference does it make?' she stopped him. 'You're nothing in all this,' she said, 'neither am I. All you've got to do is keep this place together,' she said. 'That's all you've got to do.'

'I'm doing it,' he said, blinking at her.

'That's good then. I've taped the show, if you want to see it,' she said to me. 'I'm tired. I have to go to bed. Lock up, Tony, won't you?'

We stood in silence, my dad and me, without our tea. 'She's tired,' he said. He looked at the carpet. 'She's tired,' he said again.

'I know she is,' I said.

He looked at me. He breathed in, as if to say something, but didn't say it.

'Look, Dad,' I said. 'Why don't you take that money?'

'No, I –' he reacted.

'No, Dad, listen a minute. Take that money. I don't need it. I get all my clothes for nothing. They just keep sending me stuff, hoping I'll wear it for a photograph or something, or on TV. I don't have to pay to go anywhere – I never go anywhere. Tomorrow's Sunday, I'm rehearsing. I don't need any money, Dad. Take it. Use it on the house. Buy some stuff. Use the money, Dad. I don't want it.'

Six

'Brilliant! Real coup! The girl done good! Fantastic! I wouldn't have! Ha ha!' Ray in a rail, bursting forth across the studio, deep joy, light unlimited. Two days, two days only, since I'd made my announcement on Frank Fisher, Ray had reversed, burst out all hope and glory like a mad disc-jockey football manager. 'Brill! Couldn't have done it! You a! Fan-friggin-tastic!'

Then there's me, back in favour for accidentally re-kickstarting the sales of *If Ever* by threatening to walk away. Brill! Fan-everything-tastic! Telephone calls to Ray's office come lunchtime Monday confirmed the queues at the record shops demanding copies of my CD and vid. It was as if my drawing away from publicly performing the song suggested that it was about to be withdrawn entirely.

'Don't give 'em what they want!' Ray declared. 'That gets 'em wanting it!'

We were still at Number One and unlikely to be shifted this week or next – maybe not the week after that, or the week after that. Nobody knew. At this rate, we were going to be there all year. *The Word on the Street* was also being demanded, expected to shelter in the second-highest spot as long as *If Ever* stayed lodged at the top.

'You!' Ray launched himself, rugby-tackling me. He pinned me to the floor as the dancers and sound technicians looked on. 'Little genius. You don't know. Haven't a clue, you. Wanna fight?'

'Yeah,' I said, pinned down.

He laughed, letting me up. 'Friday. Be ready. Chart Toppas. *Word on the Street*. Ready?'

'I'm ready,' I said, spoiling for a fight.

'Ready?' he said, to the four dancers as they stood looking on.

One nodded. Two boys, two girls. One boy nodded. So nice. Nodded. They weren't ready. We'd only just met. But that boy gave Ray what he wanted. That's what everybody did, with Ray. Everybody except me. Except, everything I tried not to give, he took, or it just came to him. One way or the other, every way was Ray's.

'I'd like to bring a friend, though,' I said. 'No, a couple of friends.'

Raymond fixed a look on me. 'Friends? No. No friends. Family I've done. Done it. Been everywhere. All over. No friends.'

'Why not?' I said.

The sound techs and the old roadies ducked, suddenly finding so much to do. Ray's glance around the rehearsal studio seemed to clear it of almost all the personnel, except the dancers and me. The dancers probably didn't know any better – they were quite new. Me? I was spoiling for a fight, anyway.

'I said not,' he said.

'That's not a reason,' I said.

Raymond looked over at the dancers. 'Excuse me,' he said. 'Excuse me' usually sounds very polite. From Ray Ray it comes at you like an order, very nearly a threat.

The dancers, new as they were, seemed to get the message. The one that had nodded, the olive-skinned boy, turned and walked away. The other boy and the two girls followed.

Raymond stood silently studying the floor. The place looked deserted. He didn't look at me for a long time. He made a kind of tutting sound: breathed in, out, long and hard. 'You . . . ah,' he said. Then said nothing for another long time. 'You,' he said again, eventually, 'lucky girl, yeah? You don't need to answer. Listen. Luck runs out, right? If I were you.' He shook his head. That tutting sound came out of him again. 'I wouldn't push it. Know what I mean? Don't answer. I don't need answers. Even more, I don't need questions, yeah? Don't question me. Don't question me.'

He looked up, looking directly at me. 'When I say no, no. Yes? No, yeah? Shut up! Don't! Family and friends, no. All that, ended. This isn't.' His body position changed to face me, as if I were about to be attacked, physically. If I hadn't been me, and valuable to him, if I was another roadie or soundie or dancer, I'd have been afraid. 'No room for all that,' he said, his dark brow lowered in threat. 'And never question. Especially,' he said, indicating left and right with his head, 'especially. Never! Right? Answer!'

'I don't know what to say,' I said.

'Say "Yes, Ray".'

'Yes, Ray.'

'Now. On with the show, right? Frank Fisher's hard lessons – let this be one.'

He turned and stalked away on long cowboy legs, having gunned me well and truly down. Ray was good. When Ray make it happen, it happen. Be in no doubt. Ray turned on you, he turned you down, beat you down, did it until you were done down. I needed my mum to help me handle him. When she said no to him as she did on Saturday night – No! Capital N, with the schoolteacher in her voice – I caught a glimpse, fleetingly, of an abject school bully reprimanded by a higher, more powerful authority. I didn't have any of that.

Nobody here did. He left me, if not close to tears, then not far enough away to be altogether sure of keeping my promise: no more tears.

Conversations started to break out, tentative laughter covering the embarrassed silence.

'I'm going to have to watch out for him,' a voice came, but gently, from beside me.

I hadn't noticed his approach, the boy dancer with the ever-so-slightly brown skin and the wide, open white smile. 'Yes,' I said, forcing a smile against his smile, with his perfect teeth and huge brown eyes. 'He's a – he likes to get his own way.'

'And everyone else prefers to give it to him,' he said, glancing at the sound and lighting technicians re-emerging.

'Well,' I said, 'it's easier for them. They just do as he says. It doesn't matter. Most of the time he isn't here. Most of it gets done without him. It's better.'

'Yes, but you don't do what they do. You put up a pretty good fight.'

'Yeah? You reckon?'

'I reckon,' he said, smiling. 'So does everyone else. What you did after that Frank Fisher show, they think you're a –'

'How do you know what I did after the show?'

He smiled more broadly. I had to look at him more closely. He wasn't that tall, for a dancer.

'You're a living legend round here,' he said, glancing at the studio staff again. 'You've done so much of what you've done without Raymond. In spite of him. They really like you. Don't you know?'

I had to take a good look round the studio myself. Lovely Leo flapped at me from across the other side. Brenda, in headphones, permanently clipboarded, nodded at me once, as if she could see why I was looking at her. The crew looked and laughed, and looked again.

'See?' he said, this one dancer in his tight white vest and baggy combats. 'See what I mean?'

I looked again. The crew approved of me as I glanced at each in turn. Most of them had hardly ever spoken to me but nodded, single nods of affirmation. I'd done something that they'd appreciated far more than I had. I didn't feel like crying any more. I had to laugh instead.

'See?' he said, raising his eyebrows under his short dark hair. 'Listen,' he said, glancing over his shoulder conspiratorially, 'You want to get a couple of friends into Toppas on Friday?'

'You were listening?' I said.

He laughed. 'We all were, don't worry. You couldn't see anyone, I bet, but we were all there. We're all ears.'

But he had such perfect little ears parked either side of his lightly brown face. Some of the smoking roadies might have been of the all-ears, or all-nose, or all-belly type, but not him.

'We have to hear,' he said, speaking very closely, only centimetres from my face. 'It's what people do around here. It's how they survive. You wanna know something?'

'Yes,' I said. Yes, yes, I did indeed want to know something, standing there with the gentle sheen of his face so close to my own. I had thought this boy dancer was new – what did I know?

'They listen to you, people. You've got something.'

I could feel myself breathe in suddenly, unexpectedly.

'You just need to use it right, right? It's like getting things done. There's always a way, there is,' he said, nodding. Sweet, that little nod, as if I wouldn't have quite believed him without it. 'You want two friends to Toppas Friday? That's not Raymond Big Raymond. That's me, that is.'

'You?' looking right at him.

'Me,' he nodded. 'Give me their names, I'll see what I can do.'

'How can you?'

'I know the man. *The* man. *He* isn't it, your man. This is my man. *The* man. Tell me who you want to get in.'

'Rebecca – Beccs Bradley and Kirsty McCloud.'

'Beccs Bradley and Kirsty McCloud. OK,' with another little nod, 'leave it with me. I'll let you know.'

He nodded once again before allowing me to leave him to it. He didn't do anything – anything but dance, that is – but dance he did. We, all the studio staff and me, were rehearsing *The Word on the Street* for the show. Four dancers this time, V-formations of course, but at least these weren't a bunch of teeny girls supposed to be my mates. At least I had boys there as well – good dancers too, from what I could tell. I had to work really hard to keep up with them. They moved, as fluid as water. They were beautiful, all four of them.

He didn't do anything but dance, that dancer, but how he danced! I found myself falling in with him, following after him, copying him, learning from him. My dance tutor came and went, watching me as I watched him, smiling to herself, job done.

'Job done,' he came over and said a little later. 'Beccs and Kirsty, they're in.'

'How?' I said. He hadn't done anything, not even a telephone call, as far as I could tell.

'Don't ask,' he said, 'and I won't lie to you. I won't lie to you anyway. I just won't tell you anything you don't need to know. They're in, that's all. All they have to do is turn up.'

'Thank you,' I said.

'You want some coffee?' he said.

'No, I – I'll have water.'

'Sure. I'll get it.'

I waited for him to bring the water. I watched him walk. He walked, he even stood like a dancer, with such grace and fluidity, holding out the plastic bottle to me.

'Water,' he said.

I took the bottle. 'Thanks.'

'That's OK. My name's Jagdish, by the way. In case you didn't know.'

I didn't know. People came and went, so many people with so many different names. 'Mine's Amy,' I said, 'in case you didn't know.'

He laughed. 'Jagdish Mistri.'

'Jagdish Mystery? Wow! Great name.'

'Yeah. Amy Peppercorn. Wow!'

'Yeah, but Jagdish Mystery. Fantastic!'

'Actually,' he said, lowering his voice, bringing his face closer to mine, 'my real name's Jagdish Smith. My dad's called Harry Smith. My mum's called Iqballa Mistri. Mistri – em, eye, ess, tee, are, eye. I thought it sounded better than Smith, for a dancer.'

'It does,' I said. 'It definitely does.'

'Yeah. And, Amy Peppercorn? That your real name?'

'My dad's called Tony Peppercorn. My mum's Jill – she's a Peppercorn too. So are my little sisters. We're a whole bunch of Peppercorns.'

'You're a whole bunch on your own,' said Jagdish Mistri, dancer, arranger of admissions mystery.

His face was still close to mine. Very close, like the weather, suddenly, so close and warm I felt my stomach go, as if there wasn't enough air to satisfy my racing heart.

***

Text, received that evening, on my way home:

'C U 2MORO. JAG.'

Text to Beccs:

'GOOD NEWS! CALL U 2NITE. A.'

***

At home, not early but earlier than my mum. New furniture. 'Do you like it?' – my dad.

A new three-piece suite, white leather. I hated it. 'It's – it's –'

'Fantastic, isn't it?' he said.

The girls were sliding over the leather cushions like plump pink dusters.

'What do you think of the table and chairs?' my dad was running across the room, asking. 'Look, four legs on the table *and* on each chair.'

'It's lovely, Dad. Did Mum choose the suite with you?'

'She hasn't got the time, she says. Leave it to me. I know what we want. I've ordered new carpet too, all right?'

'Not white though, eh?'

'Of course not white. What do you take me for? Those letters are for you, by the way.'

There was a sack. A mail bag, stuffed full to overflowing, falling out over the soon-to-be-replaced carpet. 'All that?' I said. 'Is that all for me?'

'That's what's been sent here,' he said. 'The rest is at Solar. They'll deal with them. You just sign that heap of photos, put all the letters you don't want to answer with them. Ray'll soon deal with them.'

There was a knock on the door, a ringing on the bell, another, louder knock. 'That'll be –' my dad said, going out.

I picked out a handful of letters. Sitting at the table like my mother, I opened them at random, reading: 'Dear Amy . . .',

'Dear Amy Peppercorn . . .', 'Dear Ms Peppercorn . . .', 'To Amy . . .', 'Amy . . .', 'Hell To Pay'.

Hell To Pay?

I held the letter closer, reading Ben's lyrics again, in his own handwriting:

Hell To Pay

Whatever you do it's insane,
You can't look back
Locked in the right-hand lane,
You're on the wrong track.
What have you done?

Wherever you're going to
Keep your heel to the floor.
It's all over now, baby, for you,
They can't touch you any more.
What have you done?

Where can you go
In the light of the truth
When the only thing you have
Is your light and your youth
When your dreams are all on fire
You have nothing
But your hot wires
And your desire.
Keep your heel to the floor
It's all over now
They can't touch you any more.
What have I done?

There, in Ben's awkward, angular handwriting, that last changed line: What have I done?

What had he done? Geoff's life over and done. Ben's? I didn't know. How could I? Looking at the prison-brown envelope with my name and address handwritten by someone other than Ben, with my tears blurring the ink of my address, how could I, what could I know?

There was nothing else inside the envelope, no return address for Ben. Nothing for Ben. Sending texts meant trying to communicate with nothing. Like sending texts to Geoff.

'What's the matter?' my dad said, bouncing in with the girls in his arms. 'Amy? Are you all right?'

'A,' went Georgie.

'Me,' said Jo.

I looked up, in tears. 'What did they say?'

'A' – George.

'Me' – Jo.

'Amy,' my dad said, beaming at them in turn. 'They say it between them, don't you, girls?'

'Poo!' they both said, squeezing his nose.

They forgot my tears. I tried to. I hid them from my mother, tucking them away in my breast pocket, as she came in late from work.

'Mummy!' my dad declared.

As the girls scrambled for her, their mummy, blinking in disbelief at the new three-piece suite, was saying, 'What on earth's that?'

'Poo!' the little girls said.

'Oh, poo!' I said, leaving them to it as my mother mocked incredulously at white settee and armchairs, at the idiocy of my dad as he ducked, hiding behind my sisters, who started crying again.

I felt like crying again. The buff brown envelope and the nastiness of Ben's writing paper coloured all my pictures of him, locked up, brown-papered, prison-suited, shut far away. A text message I didn't send said 'Your dreams are all on fire.'

His dreams, his papers burned in my hands to a cinder. I was going to call Beccs, to tell her about Friday, about 'The Chart Toppas Show'. I was going to let myself feel generous, positively magnanimous by inviting Kirsty too. No hard feelings. I was supposed to be a star, with no time for silly schoolgirl grudges. Everything was supposed to be going my way.

Downstairs the telephone was ringing. There were raps and rings on the front door. My mum was decrying my dad loud enough to be heard over and under the wailing of my dear little sisters, loud enough to be heard by everyone in the street or rapping to be let in our front door.

Ben had hell to pay. I was holding his letter in my hands, crumpling it, grinding it, mashing it into a ball and throwing it against my bedroom window.

'Dear Amy,' my mail read. 'Dear Amy Peppercorn . . .', 'Dear Ms Peppercorn . . .', 'Hell To . . .'

I'm still paying too. I can't stop.

My dad was trying to defend himself: 'Well, why don't you come with me then, if you dislike it so much? How'm I supposed to know?'

'You know I don't have time though, don't you?' my mum screeched back at him. 'And how much did it cost?' she wanted to know. 'How much does white leather cost?'

'Amy doesn't mind,' he tried to say.

'No!' she screamed. 'But I do!'

I am still paying too. I still have hell to pay. If only I could do it just with money. If only it were that easy.

Seven

'No, I know what she means, though,' Kirsty was saying, sitting in the back of a black limousine on the way to the 'Chart Toppas' studios. Courtney Schaeffer had been bad-mouthing me again, or so the Solar people put it, in the popular press. She'd been saying that all I was good for was covering old sad songs that old sad people wanted to buy week after week. That's how *If Ever* was still at the top, in the Number One spot, she said, after all these weeks.

Kirsty, of course, had some sympathy for her point of view. And so did I, I have to admit. 'Yeah,' I said, 'but I'm doing *The Word on the Street* tonight, which is still at Number Two, and that's not an old sad song.'

'No,' Kirsty had to admit, 'it's more like a Courtney song than anything.'

'She's always having a go at you,' Beccs turned to me and said. She'd been waving out of the window at people on the pavement as if she were one of the Queen's other daughters.

Kirsten shot up from her big padded seat in her short black skirt. 'No, I'm not!' she started to defend herself. 'I'm not always having a go! Why'd you say that?'

Beccs stared at her for a moment. 'What?' she said. 'What do you –'

'She wasn't talking about –'

'Stay out of this!' Kirsten turned on me. 'Mind your own business. If she wants to go saying things like that about –'

'Not about you!' I tried to say.

'Courtney Schaeffer,' Beccs said.

'What about her?' Kirsty said.

'Courtney's always having a go at Amy,' Beccs said, but sounding as if she was trying to change what she really meant.

'She isn't,' Kirsten said. 'She just says what she thinks. What's wrong with that? Anyway, you're always having a go at Courtney, in our paper.'

'No, she's not,' Beccs said.

'What paper's that, Kirsty?' I said.

'All the papers. You're always in the papers, saying things.'

'You know I don't say anything like half the things they write, don't you? Or do half the things they say I do.'

'Why do they say it then?'

Good question. That was Kirsten, with such an uncharacteristically good question. I didn't know why the papers wanted to say these things, or how they got the information they used. 'Amy Peppercorn: I'm better than Courtney!' That, after my appearance on Frank Fisher. 'Courtney: Little Amy's not big enough to fill my shoes!' That, the day after. Practically every day there was something. 'Little Amy: Joy-riding Delinquent – he's my boyfriend!' 'Amy Peppercorn Banned From Friend's Funeral!'

Practically every day I was following on behind some hysterical exclamation mark: 'Little Amy! Love's Labours Lost!' That crazed exclamation a prelude to some very personal suppositions about little me and the night-riding, joyriding young offender currently languishing – languishing, they said – in a secure wing somewhere in some buff-envelope hostelry in the remand-home counties.

'Why do they say it then?'

'They say all sorts of things,' I said.

'Leave her alone, Kirsty,' Beccs said. She was looking like a cousin of Kirsty's, or a sister, or some other close approximation. I wanted my friend, my best friend with me. I wished I hadn't invited Kirsty. I had wanted to appear generous, but my best friend couldn't be simply that – not quite, not entirely – with her cousin there, brushing each other's hair and checking one another's make-up.

'Tell her to leave me alone then,' Kirsty snapped, all legs and arched superior eyebrows. 'I was only saying, and the two of you are going on at me – going on at me. I wouldn't have –'

'We're not going on at you,' I said.

'She is,' Kirsty said, poking her face towards Beccs.

'I wasn't,' Beccs tried to say.

'Please don't fight,' I said. 'I can't stand it. Let's just have some fun.'

Kirsty sniffed. Beccs looked out of the window again, but didn't bother waving at anybody.

'Is that what you're wearing?' Kirsty said, looking me up and down with that incredulous expression that both humiliated and cheapened you.

'I haven't made up my mind,' I said, defending myself. 'I'll decide when we get there.'

Beccs looked back from the window. 'How can you do that?'

She hadn't hugged me tonight when I first saw her, as I was expecting her to. She'd smiled, with the long shadow of Kirsten darkening her background with a drawn curtain of long hair. From that moment I regretted inviting Kirsty.

'It's –' I said, wishing I hadn't said anything at all – 'it's all in my wardrobe, in my dressing room.'

'You've got a dressing room?' Beccs said.

'Of course she has,' Kirsty butted in. 'She wouldn't have said anything if she hadn't, would she?'

Beccs, trying to ignore her, said: 'But who chooses the stuff in your wardrobe? Where does it come from?'

'The manufacturers – you know, clothing companies, designers, exclusive shops. They just send stuff all the time.'

'You don't even have to go and buy anything?' Beccs said, her mouth open, eyes wide with wonder.

Kirsten's mouth and eyes were the opposite of her cousin's: clamped sourly closed, glancing dirtily from the corner of her slitted eyes. 'No more Shop-at-the-Top for her then,' she said.

'How do you –' Beccs said, still ignoring her – 'I mean, all your money – what happens to all the money?'

'I put it in my account,' I said. 'Or I give it to my dad. He's doing up the house. He spends much more money than I do. I don't spend any, in fact,' I said, shaking my head. 'I can't go into a restaurant anywhere and pay. They won't let me. Everything's free,' I said.

Beccs blinked in absolute wonder. Kirsten cringed, falling back into the shadows of the far corner of the limousine, falling back behind the closed curtain of her faultless hair. Anyone looking in, anyone that didn't know me, know of me from my frozen features trapped in the flash photography of the everyday journals, anyone recently from abroad or from another planet would think that gorgeous Kirsty was the young starlet and I the tomboy mate left over from school. I still felt like a fraud somehow, compared with Kirsty's long legs and Courtney Schaeffer's stage persona, her power, her presence. Ben's letter had knocked my confidence again, reminding me of what I wasn't doing, of what I wasn't able to do.

I wanted Beccs to make it all good and exciting, as she had before. Jag Mistri had told me that he wondered if I could really expect to keep my old friends. He said he wasn't sure it worked like that.

I wept in secret about that, blotting Ben's handwritten copybook, blurring everything – my past, my present, the ambition of my future. I didn't know how to cope with where I was going, away from my few surviving friends and my warring family.

'Everything's free,' Kirsty mimicked from the shadows.

'Ben wrote to me,' I said.

'Did he?' Beccs said, leaning quickly towards me.

Kirsty shimmered in the half-light.

'What did he say?' Beccs said.

'He wrote out *Hell To Pay*,' I said.

We didn't say anything. The car stopped at a set of traffic lights. Outside, a group of girls a few years younger than us were jostling and laughing on the corner, trying to see inside the car. 'Some of your fans,' Kirsty said.

I shrank. If I had to shrink much further, I'd disappear. One of these days I'd have to do just that.

'He's got a broken shoulder and broken ribs,' Beccs said. 'They might set bail for him.'

'How do you know?' I said.

'Geoff's mum told her,' Kirsty came in. 'Geoff's mum told her, at Geoff's funeral.'

***

I was looking at Beccs as if she was a long, long way away. We were sitting in the back of a limo, being driven to my dressing room in the TV studios. This should have been a good time, a celebration, a good laugh between best friends. But I felt as if I should be texting her across the dark interference that was Kirsten McCloud, rumbling and threatening like a storm cloud in a seat on her own.

'Why are you doing *The Word on the Street*?' Kirsty said,

looming forward out of the gloom, 'with *If Ever* still at Number One? Why aren't you doing that?'

'I'm not doing it any more,' I said.

'Why not?' she said, as if she hadn't seen me on Frank Fisher.

But Beccs knew why. I'd told her exactly how I felt. 'I'm just not,' I said, specifically to Kirsty, to whom I owed no explanation.

Kirsty didn't say anything.

Beccs didn't say anything either, but the unspoken communication between the three of us sparked like lightning from the storm threatening overhead. She'd always been the one in the middle, my friend Beccs, ever since Kirsty had come between us. But now, with Kirsty and me more and more diametrically opposed to one another, poor Beccs was being pulled apart from either side. Nothing I said to her she could ever repeat to Kirsty, and nothing Kirsty ever said would she be able to tell me. Beccs was in the middle, with the two sides drawing further and further apart. And all I had was my text messages and her occasional voice on the end of the phone line. I couldn't get close to her any more. Kirsty was there, getting in my way, now that she was able to do it. She was able to do it.

***

Lovely Leo came by to wish me luck. 'Ooh!' he squeezed. 'Flowers! Are these for me?' he said picking them up from the table. He quickly read the label. ' "Good Luck",' he read. ' "You won't need it. Jag." Jag?' he said, turning to look at me. 'Well, well! No flowers for Leo,' he said to Beccs and Kirsty. 'Doesn't she just make you sick?'

Beccs just smiled. 'Yes,' Kirsty said.

'She's got everything,' Leo breezed, 'hasn't she? Look at her. Isn't she just –' he sneezed – 'ooh, she's just so, so, so –' and sneezed, profusely, at Kirsty. 'Oh, sorry. Hay fever. I hate flowers, don't you?' he said, plonking them back on the table.

'Yes,' Kirsty said. Beccs just smiled.

'Anyway,' Lovely Leo curtsied, 'knock 'em dead, Kiddo! Ooh, I'm just so showbiz,' he laughed, pausing only to kiss me on his way to the door. 'Better go,' he said, without looking back. 'Wouldn't like to run into you-know-who.'

'Who?' Beccs said.

'Ray, my – you know, my manager.'

There was a knock at my dressing-room door. For a moment I froze, imagining that by saying his name I had conjured Ray Ray out of the stormy air to storm still harder on me for defying him with my friends' presence.

But Jagdish changed the atmosphere in a single moment as he danced through the door in his combats and tight white singlet. In the time it took to look at us, and we at him, he lifted the stormy oppression from us, with all of us on our feet and smiling like the three close friends we could never hope to be.

'Jag!' I said.

He came in smiling. 'Did you get my flowers?' he said, looking at me, Beccs, then Kirsty. They were looking at him – were they ever looking at him! 'Hello,' he said, smiling. 'You must be Beccs Bradley and Kirsty McCloud.'

Yes, they were, they laughed. They giggled without actually saying anything, but confirming yes, that's who they were.

Kirsty had stood up, her hair doing what Kirsty's hair did whenever there was anyone remotely male or remotely attractive anywhere near. Lovely Leo had, naturally, received not a single follicle tremor, but Jag was in receipt of the full flying mane, the blonde bombshell going off in his face.

'This is Jag,' I said to them. 'Jagdish Mistri.'

'Pleased to meet you,' Jag said, shaking first Beccs, then Kirsty by the hand.

'Jag's part of the act,' I said. 'He's a dancer.'

As I said that last part, 'He's a dancer,' I felt such a pull, a twang of pride that it must have been discernible in my voice. Certainly Kirsty started to look at me in such a way that had her hair falling ordinarily over her shoulder, dropping like her face in disappointment that I might have something to feel proud about in Jag. 'Jag arranged your passes,' I said to Beccs and Kirsty, but mainly to Beccs.

'Oh, thanks,' Beccs said, taking Jag's hand again. 'You'll be on the show then, will you?'

'Yes,' Jag smiled. 'We'll be there,' he said, 'won't we, Amy?'

On the instant, before I could prevent myself, I'd looked up at Kirsty's tightening face again. As her mouth pinched a tiny, warped smile in my direction, mine pinched one back at her.

'I love the flowers, Jag. Thanks,' I said, barely looking away from where Kirsty was looking and looking at me.

'Your tablets,' he said, still smiling. 'Where are they?'

I looked around, playing our little game. He knew I'd forget them. I knew I would, all the while I was purposely leaving them at home.

'You're hopeless,' he laughed, taking from his pocket the new tube of my tablets that I'd given him. 'Here, two tablets. Take them now. No wonder she still gets seizures,' he said to Beccs and Kirsty.

They were there as witnesses to our little act, our little ritual of playacting carer and cared-for, like a tiny new intimacy to be observed but not broken into.

I took my tablets. Jag kissed me on the cheek. Beccs watched as he did it. He'd never touched me before then. Beccs watched. I could feel Kirsty turn away.

'See you later, then,' Jag said to Beccs as he went out. He probably said it to Kirsty as well, only she was looking the other way almost entirely, pretty well permanently. Jag didn't seem to notice.

I noticed. So did Beccs. 'Jagdish Mistri!' Beccs declared. 'You didn't tell us about any Jagdish Mistri, dancer and everything!'

'And everything,' I said.

'Well, you didn't tell her about Ben,' Kirsty said to Beccs, 'so why should she tell you about her dancers?'

Beccs and Kirsty were left looking at each other now, staring, as the room resounded with the afterthump of Ben's name.

'Ben?' I said.

Beccs didn't move. She stared at Kirsty. Kirsty turned to look at me. 'She went to see him,' she said.

'You total!' Beccs said, stopping there.

'Beccs,' I said, 'did you see him?'

'Why did you have to do that?' she said to Kirsty.

Kirsty shrugged. 'Well, you did. Someone had to tell her.'

'It doesn't matter,' I said. 'Did you see him, Beccs? How is he?'

'You didn't have to do that,' Beccs said to Kirsty. Then, to me: 'I was going to tell you. *You didn't* have to do that,' she said again to Kirsty, but more venomously, with far more purpose.

'Yes, I did,' Kirsty shrugged.

'It's all right, Beccs,' I tried to say.

'No, it isn't,' she said.

'It's all right, Beccs,' Kirsten mimicked me, but over-sweetening my voice to sickliness. 'It's all right, *Beccs*!'

'You just can't,' Beccs tried to say. She was unable to say more, trembling furiously as she was.

'What's so special about her, anyway?' Kirsty said. 'What's so special about *her*?'

'Nothing,' I said.

'She's very special!' Beccs almost shouted. 'To me she is.'

'Well, not to me!' Kirsty shouted back. 'She's nothing to me. I don't know what I'm doing here, with all her designer clothes and dancers!'

'Wishing they were yours, that's what you're doing!' Beccs shouted back.

'Beccs,' I tried to calm her. They were about to start screaming. 'Beccs!'

'No. It's not all right. She's like this all the time. You're like this all the time. Why did you bother coming here tonight?'

'I wish I hadn't.'

'I wish you hadn't! You've been like this all the time! Amy wishes you hadn't come as well, I bet, don't you?'

'Beccs, don't!'

'Oh! The both of you, is it? That's how it is, is it? You both wish I hadn't come! Why invite me then?'

'Good question!' Beccs screamed. 'I can't imagine why Amy would want to invite you! I couldn't imagine why anybody would!'

'You bitch!' Kirsten screamed, lashing out.

Beccs caught hold of her arm, twisting it. I tried to get between them.

'You bitch!' Kirsten screamed. 'You've hurt my arm! You bitch! The two of you – the two of you can –' she stammered, trying not to cry. Twin tears dropped from her eyes before she could fling herself away. She was crying as she ran from my dressing room.

We stood together, Beccs and me. I turned to her. The door was open in front of us.

'She's –' Beccs started to say.

I put my arm round her.

'Ever since – she's eaten up with it. She's always going on about it. About you. I can't stand it.'

'Go after her,' I said.

'She won't come back,' she said.

I hugged her.

'Ben asked me not to tell you I was going to see him,' Beccs said. 'He's – he's so upset. He gave me this,' she said, reaching for her bag. She produced a letter, a prison brown envelope with my name printed on it in that handwriting that wasn't Ben's. 'He gave me this for you. His mum let me go and see him. She thought I was you first of all, and said no. Then she said yes. I waited for weeks. He's –' she said, with her own tears falling – 'he's all right. Not all right, but, you know – he's not the same. None of us are, are we?'

'No,' I said, hugging her as she hugged me. 'None of us are.'

Eight

Last Chance Remark

Last lines to our maniac dreams,
Lights out, love's lost in the dark.
Life isn't always what it seems
When you're racing it,
When you're hung on the last chance remark,
When you're awake and you're facing it.

You're broken down, boy.
You're the loser.
You're fortune's clown, boy,
Beggar, not chooser.
Wake up in a fit
You know what you are
Get up and run for it,
You won't get far.

There's no place to turn here
No going back, it
Has no reverse gear.
So forward madly
Till you stack it
Take what's coming
Fortune's packet,
Death defying,
But you can't hack it.

Love isn't always what it seems,
Last lines pen a maniac's dreams.
Lights out, life's lost in the dark.
When you're awake you're facing it,
You're all through with racing it,
All that's left is the last chance remark.

Nine

Ray caught me reading, crying. 'Now what? What now?'

I had to crumple the wretched sheets of Ben's letter away, to keep Ray from wrenching them from me. Enough was being wrenched from me as it was. I was losing Ben because I knew, now, that Ben was losing himself. His new song had sincerity, but a sadness I'd never seen before. It had a note of finality in the tune of it – a tune I somehow recognised without having heard. I think it must have been the left-over effect of having Ben's music so solidly fixed inside my mind that his words would subconsciously attach this easily to a tune I never knew I knew. Ben had sent me his song, his last-chance remark, and I had opened the coarse buff envelope and listened to it, the whole of it, complete.

It made me weep to hear Ben so plainly in my dressing room. The words and music of the McGregor/Fine song, my Number Two hit, meant nothing to me, never had. They meant less than nothing compared to what Ben could do to me between the lines of his last-chance remark, as desperate and as beautiful as it was.

All Ray Ray could do was stand in the doorway checking my room for uninvited guests – uninvited by him, that is. All he could do was to shout 'What now?' with his patience running out as quickly as his high temper could fly.

Beccs had had to run off after Kirsty, luckily, leaving me alone with Ben's song, his rhythm and soul searching me out in the ever-cold corner of my silent room. Jag's flowers wilted, with falling, forlorn heads, shedding petals like the pearls dropping from my eyes.

Raymond Raymond wanted to ride rough-shod over everybody else's emotions. He appeared at my door ready for a rough ride. 'What now? Now what?'

I crumpled Ben to my heart, folding my vulnerability away to deal with the bully-boy. Ray could only get to me if I let him near enough. I was learning, fast, how to keep him away. 'Don't you want tears from me any more, then?' I looked up, defiantly, to say.

'You're doing *The Word*,' he said, 'not *If Ever*. Jolly up.'

'Right,' I said. 'Jolly up. That's what I'd better do then, isn't it?'

'You better. Jolly up. Or else.'

'Or else?'

'Or else. Or else we fail. You don't fail on me. I got too much in. Just. No girl, don't. Investments, yeah?'

'Oh yeah,' I said. Investments. I knew all about the investments being made in me. Solar time and money, Solar power being spent on me mustn't be wasted, whatever the cost to the environment or to me personally. My every emotion had to be tied in, tied up, taken for a rough ride on Ray's bandwagon. And you didn't get off Ray's wagon until you were thrown. You never jumped, but were pushed, and pushed, and pushed.

He left me to jolly up. Nice term – Ray Ray to the hilt. Jolly up on Ray say-so. Ray say, it so. Jolly.

But Ben happened. From my crumpled pocket, his last, latest song, singing:

There's no place to turn here
No going back, it
Has no reverse gear.
So forward madly
Till you stack it
Take what's coming
Fortune's packet,
Death defying
But you can't hack it.

It seemed to have been written for me. For me and for Ben, for Geoffrey Fryer, too. Last lines to our maniac dreams – how Ben could still summarise me in a sweep of emotional words. Small wonder I could still hear him, his tunes coming to me quite naturally, swirling round me, spilling my tears.

That then was me, jollying up. I was jollying away when Jag came back, puzzled, having seen, he said, my friends leaving the building. He came in looking concerned, looking all the more concerned when he saw just how jolly I'd become there on my own like that.

'I'm on my own,' I said, as Ben's prison-buff, imprisoned words fell through my fingers to the floor.

'Yes,' Jag said, 'I've just seen your friends going out across the car park. What's the matter?'

I looked down for the letter I'd dropped, but couldn't see anything at all. My eyesight was swimming. I'd have had a seizure, a fit fit at this point I suppose, had Jag not been looking after me. I was just fit enough not to seize up, too well nourished, too regularly medicated. But my head was as if full of fits, my jaws seized, eyes bursting and full of the mocking squirms of tomorrow's headache.

'Amy?' I could hear Jag's voice saying. 'Are you okay?'

'What's happening?' I said. Beside me, very close, I could

feel his energy, his heat. 'I don't know what I –' I tried to say, without knowing what I was trying to say.

'Is this –' Jag said, I could hear him bending to pick up Ben's letter – 'this from him? From Ben?'

I nodded. Tears ran, itching the sides of my nose. I sniffed, wiping my face on one of my sleeves. It didn't seem to matter – there were plenty more sleeves hanging from hangers on the other side of my dressing room. There were gifts everywhere, given by people I didn't know to somebody they didn't know. It didn't matter to them.

'I read about him in the papers,' Jag said, handing the letter to me.

'Everything's in the papers,' I said. 'But they don't know. Nobody knows.'

'I do though,' he said, 'a bit.'

'No, you don't. No, you don't. I can't –' I said, but finding that I couldn't explain.

'Have your friends gone home?' he said softly.

I nodded. 'Ray wants me – you know what Ray wants, I know you do.'

He nodded too. 'We all know that, don't we? Now you've got to do the show on your own –'

'On my own. Yes. See? I'm on my own. Beccs didn't – she can't – I can't keep – she can't keep with me. She's, like, slipping through my fingers. I can't hold on. Geoff's gone. He's gone. Ben's –' I said, holding up the sheet that Jag had given me from the floor – 'Ben's this. I'm that. My dad's my dad – he doesn't know anything. He's like my sisters. They're all – all babies. My mum, she's like – she's like – as if she – doesn't even –' crying now, with Jag's heat, his listening energy so near. 'My mum looks at me as if she doesn't recognise me. And that's how I feel, Jag, that's how I feel. As if I can't recognise myself and it's not good. It's horrible,

horrible,' but with Jag's arm round me not quite, not quite as horrible as it could have been.

***

Jag stayed with me. 'It's all right,' he said. 'Listen to me. I can tell you something. You wanna know something?'

Yes, I wanted to know something. As it was, I knew nothing, being hardly able to recognise myself or my friends, or be recognised by my family. What can you know when you feel like this?

'You're confused,' Jag told me. He was right, but that was easy to see. My confusion was written all over me. 'But it won't always be like this,' he said. 'You're confused at the moment because you want your success, don't you?' He stopped, awaiting a reply.

'Yes,' I said. 'Yes, I do. I've got to.'

'No,' he said, straight away, 'you haven't got to want it. You want to want it, don't you?'

I nodded, although it didn't sound much like a question this time.

'I know you do. You want your success, but you also want your friends. You want them as they were, and your family. But you can't, because you're not as *you* were. You're different, Amy. This is another Amy Peppercorn. Things aren't the same. Everything's changed. You can't expect people to be the same towards you. If they were, you'd still be at school doing your A-levels and I'd be dancing somewhere else tonight without you. If you were the same, I wouldn't have met you. And I wouldn't want not to have met you.'

I was looking into his face as he spoke, as he gazed into mine. An easy tear slipped from the side of my nose into the corner of my mouth. Jag's finger gently touched it away, gently, gently touching my face.

'I wouldn't want that,' he said softly, his voice even gentler than his touch. 'And I hope you wouldn't.'

I shook my head so slightly, unable to speak, unable to move properly.

'All that stuff in the papers, it's all part of the game. You have to play them at their own game. Do the Courtney Schaeffer bit. Tell them how much you don't like her. No, listen, it's a game. Tell them you don't like Courtney – that you hate her as much or more than she seems to hate you. You know she doesn't, but she plays the game. She knows how to deflect the spotlight from her private life.'

'I won't have a private life left.'

He smiled, touched away another tear – the last. 'Yes, you will,' he said. 'It'll just be different. Let it all be different. Your friend got killed. There's nothing you can do about that. Your other friend's in prison.'

'On remand.'

'Whatever. He's going to need a lawyer, a good one. You could do that for him. See? See what you can do? Remember, you're not on your own. I'm with you right now, aren't I?'

'Ray's sending you away.'

'But I won't go. Not right away. Not,' he said, looking for another tear to touch, 'if you don't want me to.'

Jag didn't find another tear but touched anyway, so gently, so very softly, my new smile.

I had never done *The Word on the Street* quite like this. I'd never been keen on the lyrics. Too many Words On The Street, I'd always thought, tripping along to a nicely dancy little tune totally engineered for the V-formation, Saturday morning shopping mall routines. This time though, it was very different.

Sure, we started off in our formulated V on the little 'Chart Toppas' platform stage, but we were live. A-live. I was sparking. I was wearing very mauve hipster trousers and a little top. Did you see it? Did you see the way that new smile of mine flooded out over the 'Toppas' studio crowd as if *The Word* really was my song, sung from the heart, back on the right track?

We were supposed to run the routine from start to finish without hesitation doing what we did then coming off at the end. But I didn't care for that. I didn't care, neither did Jag. He had nothing to lose, and I was on a winning streak. We started to dance together, way out of formation. The other three dancers started, spontaneously, to have some fun. They were, after all, professional dancers. They knew how to dance. Dancers abhor the V-formation even more than I do. It's no fun for them to have to hold, to toe the line. Jag started to dance with me, some crazy thing we'd been doing together in the studio when we should have been concentrating. I started to laugh when I should have been singing, running back through the McGregor and Fine song cycle.

In an instant the routines broke, the lyric went, bursting into laughter as the dancing on the tiny stage rioted from the rote we'd all been so depressed by having to learn. It felt good suddenly. Sparks started to fly. Something special broke out, like a peal of laughter that should have been another repetitive song lyric. A cheer went up from the crowd, their hands applauding above their heads as Jag danced with me crazily on camera, live, as alive as can be.

There were no tears. The tears were all finally gone. I

laughed, sang. Tears couldn't touch me as Jag had touched and then kissed them all away. The gentle touch of his hand was hard compared to the softness of his lips brushing my cheek, pressing the tear-salt swell of my lips.

My eyes closed, I could feel the warmth of his mouth softly against mine. Eyes open, we were on the small stage driving every vestige of routine into touch, dancing and loving every second of this.

The television cameras recorded what was everything that shouldn't be done on 'Toppas', everything that Ray Ray would almost definitely be holding against me and using to drive Jag out and away from me. But we weren't having it. We were for doing what we were doing – dancing like this, throwing out one bit of lyric or the other, one line of *Word* as and when I felt like it. When I felt like it I reached down to the studio audience, helped one of the girls dancing there on to the stage. Jag reached for another. Then all we were doing was hauling people up on to the stage camera-view, dancing with them on TV, having more outrageous and unrehearsed fun than anybody, including Courtney Schaeffer, had ever had.

Ten

Text From Beccs:

'LOVED IT! LOVED IT! LOVE, BEX.'

Yes! Beccs, texting me about what Jag and I had done on 'Toppas'. Beccs, calling me, saying 'Hey! That was great! Sorry I missed it. Really sorry I missed it.'

'It wasn't your fault,' I said.

'I won't ever let her do that to us again,' she said.

I loved it when she said that, saying Us like that, keeping me with her and her with me. Jag was right – I was different, which wasn't a bad thing. In fact, it was good. It was a good thing. *I* was a good thing.

I can't tell you what a difference it made. I felt so very, very – just different. I felt light. The sparks that had seemed to come from me on the show still glinted on the ground where I'd walked, or so it seemed to me. There was an energy I hadn't felt since Car Crime did its first gig in the school hall. Not even then, really – this was different again, a thing of its own. That Car Crime gig had felt good; this felt good in its own way. I felt good in my way. I had this, this feeling, this energy, dancing, laughing, singing, involving the crowd, the audience.

'I really wanted to be there –' Beccs enthused over the phone, 'when I saw what happened. You and that dancer –'

'Jag.'

'Yeah. Hey – Jag? What about him? "Have you taken your

tablets, Amy?"' she said, mimicking him in my dressing room.

We laughed. 'I know,' I said. 'What do you think?'

'What do I think? Kirsty'd kill for half a chance. And there you are, the two of you – so – the two of you?'

I laughed. 'He's nice, isn't he?'

'Nice? You're kidding! A face and body like that? A dancer? Nice doesn't come anywhere near.'

'I know,' I said, still laughing. 'But – Beccs, what do you think? What do you think I should do?'

'Do?' she said, with amusement.

'What about Ben?' I said.

Her face straightened. 'What was in the letter?' she said.

'A song. A new song. That's all.'

She didn't say anything.

'Beccs? How was he, really?'

She didn't say anything.

'I'm going to pay for a lawyer for him. A good one. If his mum will let me.'

'That's all you can do,' she said. 'He's not your responsibility.'

'No, but I feel so – he's my friend.'

'And mine,' she said. 'But you're here, and he's there, so you can leave him to me.'

'Can I? Can I just do that, like that? After everything we –'

'I'll look after him,' she said. 'You've got too many other things to think about. You've got to do it right, if only to shut Courtney up. Did you see what she said about you in the paper?'

'Don't take any notice of that,' I said. 'It's only a game really. It doesn't matter. It just keeps the press away from all the other things you don't want them prying into.'

'Oh yes?' she said. 'And what things might they be? Anything to do with your dancer? Jag, isn't it? Anything to do with him?'

'Might be,' I said.

'Oh, yes? Tell me, tell me!'

'Nothing to tell – only – only that when he kisses you, his lips are really soft and he tastes as sweet as a peach.'

Beccs screamed.

***

I wanted to scream too, really I did. Everything felt so good all of a sudden – too good maybe. Ray Ray was going to catch up with us, blowing his red top at what we did on 'Chart Toppas', stuttering a blue murder at me, definitely getting rid of Jag. Jag said he just wouldn't go away, not right away. I hoped he was telling me the truth, but Ray would be a hard man to defy. If Ray wanted rid of someone, Ray got rid. It happen. Ray say.

That night, the night of the Toppas performance, I stayed at the McGregor/Fine mansion as it was so late. Leo dropped by. 'Listen, Lovely,' he breezed, 'we'll all be on tour very soon, as you know.'

'Soon?' I said. There had been talk of touring, but no talk of how soon. 'How soon? Nobody's told me!'

'I'm telling you now. You need to be sure you're ready,' he said.

I wasn't ready. I had to call my mum. My dad answered. 'Best just to leave her to get her sleep. She's working so hard. Hey, great show! What a laugh you were all having, eh?'

'How are Georgie and Jo?' I said.

'Fantastic,' he said. 'We let them stay up and watch the show last night. They saw it was you. They loved it.'

'Did they?' I said.

'So did your mum,' he said.

Beccs called me, interrupting my conversation with my dad. We screamed, me and my best friend. She vowed never to let Kirsty do that to us again. Things were changing ever so quickly all round me. I was changing too. It felt good all of a sudden. All of a sudden. Even saying 'all of a sudden' felt good, as if things should happen suddenly if they were any good.

I was trying to get to sleep in the M and F mansion, which wasn't easy at the best of times, when the telephone – my mobile – went again. There was too much empty room around me here to let me sleep easily; then, when I answered my mobile, there suddenly wasn't enough space to allow me a decent breath of air.

'It's me,' Jag said.

'Hello, Me.'

'Are you asleep?'

'I'm never going to sleep again.'

'I know,' he said. 'Great show. *Great* show!'

'Yeah. Our best yet.'

'Our? You seen Raymond yet?'

'No. You?'

He hesitated. 'No,' he said. 'Still, he doesn't matter, does he? We'll do what we want to do, won't we?'

'I hope so,' I said.

'Listen,' he said, 'I'd like to give you a kiss goodnight. I know I can't, but if it's all right with you, I'll give you a kiss goodnight when I see you in the morning.'

He stopped. I wondered if he could hear my breathing, or my heart beating in my mouth through the mobile telephone. I couldn't speak. I couldn't say a word.

'Is that all right?' he said. He was speaking so softly into my thundering, pulsating ear, I could hardly hear what he was saying.

'Yes,' I said, because I could and would hear what he was saying. Through it all I could hear him, but all I could manage to say was yes. 'Yes,' I said.

'See you tomorrow then,' he said.

'Yes,' I said again. 'See you tomorrow.'

'Goodnight,' and he was gone. And I was left alone in M and F world without much sleep to speak of, although that didn't seem to matter. Sometimes, when I couldn't sleep, whenever I'd been worried about something – my A-level Maths, my biology, Ben, Geoff, Kirsty, Beccs – then losing sleep was just that – just like a loss I'd have to struggle to get over. This time though, losing sleep felt like my gain. I felt so energised, so positive, so very excited.

At one point I considered getting out Ben's last letter to me again, just to bring myself down a bit. Then I realised that that would be a stupid thing to do, to try to get some sleep by worrying about Ben rather than dreaming of Jag. As if that would have worked! I'd have only been exchanging the positive energy for the negative.

Then, before I knew it, it was a new morning I was waking into, jumping out of bed still positively energised, jumping into a shower I purposely kept quite cold to try to cool myself off a bit.

Lovely Leo was already there, enjoying his lonely breakfast in that vast and empty house. I thought I was going to be the only one there, with my footfalls echoing off the expensive stone tiles of the kitchen through the under-populated halls and havens.

But Leo was glittering there over his little breakfast bowl and his fruit and his goat's milk cheese. 'My, my!' he sang. 'But aren't you the lively one this morning?'

'I'm happy,' I said, 'for a change.'

'Change indeed,' Leo said, picking cheese from his sparkly jumper. He had some beautiful clothes, Lovely Leo, with designs and colours that you just didn't see in the shops anywhere.

'Where'd you get that lovely jumper, Leo?'

'Oh, I knitted it, Sweet. Do you like it? How lovely of you to notice. Do you know, I like you so much better when you're like this.'

I did too. Much better. Even going for another day in the studio at hot and stuffy Solar, finishing off the last tracks for my first album, seemed like so much more fun. I couldn't wait to get there. We sat in the back of the car chatting all the way like girlfriends while the driver watched the road.

Ray Ray was going to get us, I knew. He was already gunning for Jag and now, after last night's performance . . . but I didn't care. I couldn't wait to get there.

Leo followed me into the building, calling after me. 'What's the hurry? Wait for me. Wait for me.'

But I couldn't wait. I practically ran in looking for Jag. I didn't feel as if I hadn't slept much. In fact, I felt as if I'd had the longest and most refreshing sleep of my entire life. I felt perfect.

Big Ron, the big-bellied studio manager, was there, fiddling over his control consoles with a pair of huge headphones on. He looked up as I cruised in, looking around.

Nothing. Big Ron only, in black T-shirt and faded black jeans, dressed, as usual, as if for an extremely informal funeral.

'Where is everybody?' I said, my eyes going everywhere.

Ron looked about, removing his headphones. 'What?'

'The place is deserted.'

Ron looked again, as if I might have been wrong. 'Who's

missing?' he said. 'Most of the work's done. Just a few bits and pieces to re-do. Other than that, it's a wrap. Only me and you needed,' he said, glancing at Leo as he came in with his knitting.

'I'll just stay over here,' Leo shrugged, as if insulted, 'out of the way, shall I?'

'Where's Jag?' I said.

'Who?' said Ron.

'You mean that dancer, don't you?' Lovely Leo interjected, nodding and pouting. 'She means that dancer.'

'Dancer?' Ron said. 'We don't need no dancers today. Not today we don't.'

'She does though,' Leo pouted. He smiled. 'Don't you worry, Lovely,' he said, nodding at something outside the studio control room. 'Look what Leo's conjured up for you.'

He laughed as I looked through the glass to where Jag was taking a packet of my pills from his pocket, holding them up. 'Have you taken them?' he mimed.

I wanted to run out there. My face was going red, flushing with embarrassment, with anticipation, with relief and joy. Jag was there, when all that was required was Big Ron and Little Amy. He looked after me with my diet and tablets, despite not being required by Solar, by Big Ron or by Ray Ray.

'He looks after my medication for me,' I said, offering Ron and Leo an explanation – I don't know why. My flushed, expectant face necessitated a few words for them, I supposed, before I went from the control console to where Jag was waiting for me.

'I haven't taken them,' I said straight away. 'I forgot. I didn't think to –'

'We'd better – shall we go and get you some water then?' Jag said, stopping me, smiling at me.

'We're – I'm just going to get some water,' I popped back into the control to say to Ron and Leo.

'It's all the same to me, Lovely,' said Leo.

'Hurry up,' snapped Ron, snagging his head with its long straggly hair back between the grip of the head-cans.

'Let's hurry up,' Jag laughed as we ran to the dirty little kitchen area where they liked to keep about fifty or so old mugs unwashed and half a dozen cartons of curdled milk in the fridge that didn't work. Jag turned on the cold tap. I waited. 'Do you want to find something decent to drink out of?' he said.

I didn't care. I shrugged. 'I don't care.'

'No,' he said, 'but I do.' He looked at me then. Looked right at and into me. 'I do,' he said again, so softly I thought he'd touched me tenderly on the spine and the back of my neck.

No one can know what that's really like. There's something wonderful in all of us, something that's only touched but rarely, specially, flooding forward as if tapped from a secret source you never knew you had. It's beautiful. You can feel it from every part of your body and being, all of you at once – a fusing together, a flood of blood and bone and sinew and nerve and brain. Jag didn't know, he couldn't understand what he did to me, speaking to me, saying that so simply in that way. Jag couldn't fully understand it, I was sure, because nobody could. Even I couldn't get to the bottom, to the heart of what I was feeling when I was so overwhelmed with feeling it.

The tap was running cold. Jag turned from the sink and took a step towards me. 'You said it was all right,' he said, 'if I kissed you goodnight this morning.'

'Did I?' I said, or tried to say. My voice wouldn't come out properly. I talked in a whisper.

'That's what you said,' he said, standing in front of me. I

could hear the cold tap running. Then I noticed that he'd actually turned it off before turning away from the sink. All I could hear was the blood rushing through my head, running and drumming at my ears. 'In fact,' he said, 'I'm sure that's what you said. Am I wrong?'

Where we stood so closely together, face to face, mine looking up, his down, but not too much, thankfully, I could feel his heat. Or mine. I felt hot, anyway, in his force field, which was exceptionally powerful. Across the ten or twelve centimetres of the air separating us, I could already feel the smoothness of his face, the soft, peach-flavoured touch of his lips.

'I'm not wrong,' he said, 'am I, Amy?'

I shook my head, but without taking my eyes from his. I couldn't take them away. I was transfixed, pinned like a butterfly to – to whatever they pin butterflies to. Whatever it was, I felt so captured, held in one place, with Jag's face moving closer.

'I didn't think I was,' he whispered. 'Or I hoped I wasn't. I really hoped I wasn't.'

I didn't think I could stand it any longer. It was like trying to resist the urge to swallow, only far, far more powerful. I could feel myself being drawn in, drawn up to Jag's face, his soft full mouth, my own to his.

But suddenly – how everything always seemed to be so suddenly happening – there came a hiss, not a kiss – an exhalation. Raymond Raymond had appeared, hissing like a baddie at the kitchen door. On the very millisecond before our lips could finish up the slow distance that had so tantalisingly separated us, the bad boy, my Mr Big-type manager, materialised at the door. He might have been the Devil, the way he appeared as if from nowhere, from nothing.

I stepped away from Jag. Ray had one of his faces on. This

one I'd seen only too often. This face was out to get someone, anyone – it didn't care. When Ray Ray face hit, it hit hard. No question.

He glared at us, at Jag and me, the two of us together, taking us in in one go, eating us up as a single morsel.

All my good and glorious nervousness departed, usurped by bad nerves and an epileptic worry for Jag, for him personally – I was *so* worried about what Ray might want to do to him. It sickened me to see Ray look at us like that, as if we deserved such venom and spite.

As I stepped away from Jag, I felt him step towards me. As Ray stood dripping poison, I felt Jag's hand touch my waist.

Raymond, noticing the movement, the gesture, dripped and exhaled at the door for a few moments more, before saying: 'The tour. Starts early. Be ready. Everyone.' He glared at us for a few moments more, then he was gone. One moment he was filling the doorway, filling the entire kitchen with enmity, the next, nothing. Gone, just like that.

I looked at Jag, he at me. I glanced back at the vacant doorway, just to be sure. Ray Ray gone. Empty open doorway.

Jag's face, smiling. My own. I didn't understand what had happened, but I didn't want to understand anything. Jag's hold tightened on my waist, pulling me to him. I didn't want to understand, couldn't have understood, anything. Anything at all.

'We're going on tour,' Jag said.

Eleven

'A!'

'Me!'

One stood up, tottered over, the other following close behind. Neither was able to stop until they bumped into my knees and flopped backwards, laughing, onto the new carpet.

The new carpet was so deep the girls could fall without injury. It was so red, my dad could bleed all over it and nobody would be any the wiser.

'A!' 'Me!' the girls cried, but laughing.

'Georgie! Jo!' I cried back, putting down my bags, falling to my knees in the deepest carpet I'd ever felt. I didn't have far to go to kneel. I'd have to practically wade through the pile. The twins did brilliantly, tottering across this surface, even falling down as frequently as they did.

My dad came over and gave me a kiss through the tangle of the twins hanging round my neck.

My mum appeared at the kitchen door.

'Dad!' the twins cried.

'Mum!' I said, going to her. She kissed me. As I hugged her, she felt different, thinner. 'You've lost weight, Mum,' I said.

'Has she?' my dad said, looking over.

So far, my mum hadn't said anything. 'How would you know?' she said to my dad now. 'Since when did he ever notice anything?' she said to me. 'You were enjoying yourself on the show last night.'

'I don't have time to notice anything,' my dad was smiling, looking up into all corners of the room.

'Mum,' I said, 'it was great.'

'What do you think?' my dad was saying, still looking around. 'Different?'

Different, yes. The whole place was changing – furniture, fittings. All the doors had been replaced.

In the kitchen, huge lengths of heavy translucent polythene hung down where the back wall used to be. 'That'll be the extension,' my dad said.

'Because you wouldn't have realised,' my mum said, from the strange opening of the doorway, 'if he hadn't told you, would you?'

'I'm only saying,' he said, deflating slightly. 'Look,' he cried, re-inflating himself almost immediately. 'The doors fit and everything,' he said, shifting my mum. 'They close – look.'

'And open,' she said, tugging the door from him. 'How about that, Amy? The doors open and close.'

'They didn't before,' he said.

The girls were scrambling across the kitchen floor for the polythene wall and the playground of the little building site beyond in what had been our back garden. They'd forgotten that they could walk, such was their excitement at having got this close to their paradise.

'No you don't,' my dad dashed, hoisting them up by their denim dungarees. They laughed and kicked, flying like toy aeroplanes over the new kitchen table.

'They've changed,' I said. 'They would have screamed and cried at that before.'

'Everything's changed,' my mum said, but too softly, speaking almost as if to herself, with the rest of the family overhearing her.

'Are you okay, Mum?' I asked, following her into the living room.

'Me?' she said, looking up. 'I'm all right. There's nothing wrong with me. I'm just not sure,' she said, hesitantly, 'that you should – that we should be spending your money like this.'

'I don't mind,' I said.

'I've told her you don't mind,' my dad said, blundering in, rolling the girls before him like hedgehogs. 'I've told her that. She doesn't listen to me.'

'I've got nothing else to spend it on,' I said, quite truthfully, standing in our changed house wearing changed clothing neither of my parents had ever seen till now.

'Designer!' my dad declared, picking up on what I was thinking. 'Cool!' he said, dead uncool in his skinny jeans and his chubby-jowled unshaven face.

My mother turned away, looking for something on the side until the new CD/DVD player affronted her. She faltered, I could see from her reflection in the black plastic of the player, looking at my own darkly reflected image watching her. We looked at each other for quite a few moments through the dark depths, with a cloud hanging between us. I seemed to stand out here in the light, she delving into a faraway dimness.

'DVD, CD, vinyls, minis – the works,' my dad said, having mistaken my look into the surface lid of the player. 'All this is yours, Ames,' he said, spreading his arms. 'All yours.'

He let go of the smoked plastic lid, which fell gently back into position of its own volition. In it, his reflection up close, distorted big nose and teeny eyes. In his background, just me. My mother wasn't there. I looked round. She was sitting lost in the long length of the white-walled settee, looking at the twins.

'My tour starts earlier than I thought,' I had to say, severing the dry facts from the feelings.

The information didn't seem to make it as far as my mum.

'How much earlier?' my dad surfaced to say.

The girls were silent, trying, as they were, to fit a whole hand into one another's mouth.

'Much,' I said.

'How much?' my mother said.

'Tomorrow,' I said.

'Tomorrow?' my dad said.

My mum was looking and looking at me. Nothing more than that. 'Why's that?' she said.

'They've changed the tour dates,' I said. 'Added a few more, re-arranged some others. Twelve more in all. They want us everywhere. We have to start Sunday,' I said.

'Oh well,' my dad said.

My mum discussed it no further, but sat staring across the room at nothing, ignoring the fact that I was going away for weeks on end, leaving her. I had to try to make it seem as if I didn't want to, although the early tour was the best thing that could have happened. We'd need to leave tomorrow, which meant that Ray Ray wouldn't have time to replace Jag. That's what we supposed, anyway, because Jag was still with us. He was still with me, totally with me. I wanted to scream. I wanted to sing, to laugh. I felt like – as if things were so suddenly very different for me. So suddenly – there it is again, this so suddenness that wanted to change my life in so many radical ways, putting a scream, a song, a smile in my heart, but a seriousness on my face to match my mother's as she looked, unsmiling, across the room at her eldest daughter, who was going away.

'All over the country,' I said to Beccs.

'But how can they book it all up so quickly?' she said.

I laughed. 'I don't know. Radio. Solar just put it out. It just happens that quickly. Ray Ray, you know.'

'I could come and see you,' she said, genuinely excited for me, 'whenever you're anywhere near, couldn't I?'

I loved her. It was so good to have her here with me on my last night at home for such a long time. And it was so very good to have her here without Kirsty. Kirsty was still her friend – just – but couldn't be mine. We both knew this and understood it. Our friendship, Beccs's and mine, was all the stronger for it. She'd told Kirsty that whatever happened, *whatever*, she'd never stop being my friend. She didn't say best friend; she didn't need to. Special friends are what we were and always would be.

She was genuinely excited for me, as if she was coming with me everywhere I went. Well, I'd make sure she did that as much as I possibly could. Beccs would share my experiences, as I would share hers.

She'd already told me about Ben. She told me how different he was. He was not the same person, she said, holding back the tears we freely shed when I showed her the song he'd written and sent to me:

Love isn't always what it seems,
Last lines pen a maniac's dreams.
Lights out, life's lost in the dark
When you're awake you're facing it
You're all through with racing it
All that's left is that last chance remark.

'That's exactly what I mean,' Beccs cried, wiping the tears from her eyes. 'That's how he is, exactly.'

'I want to see him,' I said, placing Ben's letter safely under my mattress.

'He won't,' Beccs shook her head. 'He can't face you. He told me.'

'Why can't he face me?' I said. 'Why me?'

'He feels guilty for you,' Beccs said.

'But why particularly for me? Why me?'

'Don't you know?' she said, with the askance tilt of the question written on her sidelong face. 'You two were a bit . . . for a while, weren't you?'

'We were a bit? A bit what?' I said.

'You know,' said Beccs, smiling, but trying not to. 'A bit . . . you know.'

One of the new doors slammed downstairs. One of our old windows shook, yet to be replaced.

I got up and closed my bedroom door. I didn't want anybody overhearing our silences, the trying-not-to but smiling broadly secrets Beccs and I were about to share.

'You weren't as good at hiding it,' Beccs said, 'as you thought you were.'

'Yeah,' I said, 'I know. But, you know, I didn't think there was anything to hide. I thought – it felt as if it was just me.'

'It wasn't, though,' she said. 'It was Ben too.'

'Yes,' I said. 'But he only kissed me once.'

'Once?'

I nodded.

'Once was it? How was it?' She was smiling.

I shrugged. 'You know, it wasn't like anything. I kind of –' I glanced at my bedroom door. 'We were in the hall,' I said, 'when he kissed me. But my mum and dad were – you know, and the twins were screaming. Beccs, I can't tell you what it was like. I missed it. It was all over before it really got started.'

'Like Car Crime,' Beccs said.

'Or like Ben himself,' I said. 'Just a waste.'

'And Geoff,' we both said together, looking at each other.

'And that was it,' I said, drawing to a close everything that had happened between Ben and me.

Beccs thought about it. I could see it all flowing through her mind, events expressing themselves in the line of her brow.

'I'm paying for a good lawyer for him,' I said, 'if his mum lets me.'

'She'll let you,' she said.

A door slammed downstairs. We went quiet for a while, before another smile swept Beccs's face upwards.

'Ben kissed you and you missed it,' she said. 'But I bet you didn't miss anything when your dancer kissed you, did you?'

'I didn't miss a thing,' I smiled.

She beamed. 'Tell me. Tell me everything.'

'I'll always tell you, Beccs,' I said. 'Everything,' as she huddled down, smiling and excited, almost as much as I was myself. 'I'll always tell you everything,' I said again, before telling her all that I couldn't allow my mother to know, now that I was no longer a schoolgirl, no longer a little child. I was, in fact, no longer *her* little girl. Everything, the all I had told my friend there in my childhood's bedroom, was of a passion that suddenly – all of a fantastic sudden – had welled up in me, spinning me round and round, dizzying me, lifting me up, frightening me with its height and speed and exhilarating sense of danger.

'Yesterday morning,' I told Beccs, knowing that she wouldn't tell my mum, 'he kissed me. Jag kissed me like – like – like –'

I couldn't think what it was like when Jag kissed me, because it wasn't like anything. I'd never been there before, never experienced such feelings and emotions. I was totally incapable of comparing them to anything. He took my breath away.

'He took my breath away,' I said.

But he also took my head, my reason, my senses, my heart.

'I've never –' I said, looking at Beccs, floundering, looking for words. 'I don't – have the words,' I had to say. 'Beccs, I'll tell you everything, but I can't tell you anything. It was too – just too fantastic.'

'Where were you?' Her face was full of my secondhand joy, as she really was experiencing some of this with me.

'We were in this dirty little kitchen in the studio. Horrible little place, but it didn't matter. I could have been anywhere. It was just –' I stumbled again, slowly shaking my head, 'too much.'

'His name's Jagdish, isn't it?' Beccs said.

'Yeah. Jagdish Mistri.'

'He's a dancer,' Beccs said, not because I might not know, but just because she wanted to say it.

'And so fit,' I said.

'With a dancer's body,' she said.

We looked at each other, both trying not to burst into wild laughter.

'So fit,' I said again.

We burst out, Beccs and me, reaching out for each other in the altered atmosphere of my old, unredecorated bedroom. We laughed and laughed, ensuring that we understood each other better than anyone else in the whole world. Nothing could ever separate us, not when we were like this.

'Come on,' I said, throwing open my over-packed wardrobe doors. 'For goodness' sake try on some of this designer stuff. I'll never wear it all. I've got enough stuff to keep us both going for the rest of the year.'

'Wow!' she exclaimed, dragging out some of the teensy tops and short skirts the designers had sent me. 'Too sexy! I can't wear this stuff.'

'Take some for Kirsty then,' I said.

'No way,' she said. 'We can't wear sexy stuff like this round here. We'd never get away with it. We're not pop stars, you know. Look at this,' she said, holding up a micro-skirt in leather with tassels on one side. 'We couldn't do it. You can, but we can't, not round here.'

Twelve

So it was time to go away. 'Is that all you're taking?' my dad said. My mum was saying next to nothing, as if there was nothing to say next. But my dad was jabbering away with the twins, all three of them learning new words every day.

'Poo-the-noo!' he was saying with Georgie and Jo. 'That's Scottish,' he declared to anyone bothering to listen. 'They're bi-lingual, aren't you, girls? Is that all you're taking?' he turned and said, noticing the smallest suitcase I'd picked from the nest of new leather luggage he'd been out and bought with some more of my money. 'So many clothes upstairs,' he said, 'and that's all you're taking?'

'So many clothes wherever I go,' I had to say, trying, under my mother's eye, not to sound boastful. She hadn't said anything, hadn't accused me of being boastful or anything like that, but her distant silences suggested disbelief, or disapproval of what I was doing and what my dad was doing. She wasn't talking the Scots-poos with my sisters or clothes and radio-play with me, any more than she was screaming at my dad. But he was at her, at what she wasn't bothering to say, or saying in the smallest, most silent voice I'd ever failed to hear her use.

I wanted to get away. The car came for me and I was relieved to be going, to be driven to the hotel where I was to spend my first night away.

It was going to be exciting – far more exciting than staying at home or in the stripped halls of the M and F mansion. We were going live all over the country. My first tour. It's very unusual, so everybody kept telling me, to be headlining on your very first tour. I'd done well, everybody kept telling me, very well. Everybody but Ray Ray, that is. He didn't count as part of everybody. He was one on his own. There couldn't have been two Ray Rays, however much he might have sounded like a couple of similarly named people.

This was going to be good, I kept telling myself. Jag was going to be there after today, along with the rest of the crew. Tonight I was on my own. Tomorrow, Jag.

'What are you going to do?' Beccs had asked me in my bedroom, huddled round our excitement, hunkered down with me.

'Do?' I'd said.

'He'll be there, with you, every night.'

We laughed. He'd be there with me, in the same hotel with me. What would I do?

Beccs had become suddenly serious. 'No, really,' she said, 'what *will* you do?'

I didn't know what I'd do. Beyond the thrill I felt in my lower stomach, beyond the swirl of my swimming head, I couldn't think.

'Be careful,' Beccs said, because she was my friend. She was not my mother, therefore Beccs's careful would obviously be a whole lot more reckless than my mother's careful could ever be.

But my first night away was alone in Manchester with just my mobile and the recollection of how I felt when Beccs refused to take any of my designer clothes. The more I tried not to think of it like that, the more I couldn't help feeling how separated from her I was about to become. My mobile lay there on the hotel bed with its lights out. Its dark silence reminded me of my mum, becoming more and more uncommunicative as I moved away up country to pursue my career. I was here on my own to ensure that I, above everybody else concerned with the tour, was rested, ready for tomorrow. But I was alone here, wearing my girl-singer designer wear to bed, as I didn't have time all day to try to get a wear out of everything. Most of my dinner still lay untouched over on the table in my huge room. The staff downstairs had treated me like some kind of royalty, with a respect that isolated me from every normality they shared with each other and with every other guest in this flashy hotel.

Nobody was there with me. All my excitement seemed to have dropped out of the bottom of my small suitcase. There were flowers waiting for me in my room, as in every room, seemingly until the day I died.

If Beccs had taken some of my wardrobe away with her, I'd have called her there and then. But she hadn't, so, for some connected reason, I didn't. I suppose I knew she'd be with Kirsty tonight and our conversation would be strained, with her cousin glowering in the background like the low light from my too-silent mobile.

I reached for my phone to call my mum. For a moment, I toyed with the idea of talking to her about finishing my education when my singing career was over. But before I could get to my mobile, a door slammed in the hotel corridor. It made me jump. I listened out for voices, hearing only a restrained silence, as if my mum still wasn't saying anything.

Besides, I didn't want to see an end to my singing. I wanted to be successful, purposely, now I had accidentally stumbled into it. There was fun to be had here, such excitement that I'd never felt until – until now, when I couldn't keep it, couldn't contain it on my own without . . . without . . .

My telephone lit up at that very moment, playing the tune I'd programmed to recognise a call from the very person I'd feel so lost and alone without. My mobile sang a song of Jag, lighting up with me, allowing me to want to live a crazier, more reckless life beyond the A-level failure of my old self.

'I hope I didn't wake you,' his voice said.

'You didn't, but I wouldn't mind.'

'No,' he said, 'but I would.'

His voice, even across the bad and stuttering mobile line, made me feel light-headed, ever so slightly dizzy.

'And so would Raymond,' he said.

'Well, I don't care about him,' I said.

'Do you care about me?' he said, quite simply.

When you're not expecting such a question, but as soon as it comes it becomes the very thing in the world you most wanted to be asked, you're bound to stumble over it. I did, anyway. I nearly choked on it. My breath went from under me.

The line clicked. 'Are you still there?' Jag's voice said.

'I'm still here.'

'You didn't answer me.'

'No,' I said.

He seemed to wait, then give up. 'Are you looking forward to tomorrow? To the first gig?'

'I do,' I said.

'You –'

'Care about you.'

There was a pause. The telephone line seemed to have cleared, as I could hear my own breathing much more obviously above the line interference. Again, my telephone told me nothing for a long – for too long a time. The breathing pause ended with Jag's incoming call playing his tune massively, straight into my ear.

I dropped my mobile. It bounced on the hotel carpet, its battery flinging out in the opposite direction. The last pause had been the line cutting off. I'd lost contact with Jag again, not knowing what he'd heard or missed of what I'd been trying to say to him.

Driving my battery quickly back into place, I called him back. 'What happened?' he said.

'Bad line,' I said.

The line went dead.

'Amy?' Jag's voice, across a perfect connection, still unexpectedly live. 'You have to get to bed soon, I expect.'

'It's only nine o'clock,' I said.

'Nearly half-past,' he told me. 'You'd better sleep. You have to be fresh for tomorrow.'

'You sound like Raymond,' I joked.

He didn't seem to get it. There was no reply. 'It's just –' he started to say, as if he was taking my poor joke far too seriously.

'It's just a joke,' I said.

He paused again. 'Are you OK?' he said.

'I'm – yes, I think I am. Nervous. I don't feel quite right. Something's still not right with me.'

'It will be,' he said. 'Trust me. Do you trust me?'

'I trust you,' I said truthfully.

'Good. That's good. Trust me, Amy. I'll take care of you. Have you taken your medication?'

'Yes.'

'Good girl.'

'Good girl?' I said, laughing. 'Now you sound like my dad.'

'Oh, no,' he laughed. 'But I will, if necessary. You need to go to bed. I'm going in a minute.'

'Why don't you call me when you're in bed?' I dared to say.

'No,' he said, 'not tonight. You have to sleep. So do I. I'll see you tomorrow, then I'll give you a kiss goodnight. I always seem to have to kiss you goodnight in the morning, don't I?'

'Well, you have so far.'

'It won't always be like that,' he said. 'One day, I'll kiss you goodnight properly. Can I, one day?'

***

Watching Lovely Leo, it became apparent that he didn't actually know what he was supposed to be doing. He got in people's way; he wound them up. He interfered. He sang lots of little songs that he might or might not have made up, for all I knew, but each one had some kind of relevance to what was going on at the time:

Hello, young lovers,
Wherever you are.

Always laughing, always *that* far away from another flurry of tears.

Oh, I like women
Like women like men
So why don't women like me?

That was a song, by the way. One of dozens Leo would spring out of nowhere to sing. I sang too. I rehearsed – we rehearsed for our first gig, in Manchester, tonight. This was going to be different from anything I'd ever done. I'd done live performance, but not a whole concert-full of performance. There was a whole lot to it.

We knew what we were going to do, with Leo begging us to

go through it again and again. But because I hadn't really rested at all last night after Jag's call, my lack of sleep kept slowing my movement against those of the other dancers. 'You can do it,' Jag had to keep telling me.

He told me that so often, I had to believe him. I had to believe Jag; he was essential. He kissed me goodnight in the morning, encouraging me through Lovely Leo's rehearsals. Jag told me when to stop. He knew when. 'It's feeling it that's important now,' he said to me, with Leo in a flap at my elbow.

Jag and I shared a late lunch of fish and salad and fresh fruit. 'Your tablets,' he said, laying them out on my plate. 'How do you feel?'

'I'm okay,' I said.

'Okay's no good,' he said. 'We've got to work on you. You're going to need more than okay if we're going to be better than that. Okay?'

'Yes, okay,' I had to say, feeling better than that already, really – a lot better than that. Jag was exactly right for me, exactly right. I loved to say his name: Jagdish Mistri, which was Jagdish Smith really, but really such a mystery to me. His knowledge, like his dancing, left me standing.

'Don't worry about your mum,' he said. 'Don't worry about Beccs. They wouldn't want you to, I know.'

He said things like that as if he'd always been there with me. He talked as if he knew me so well, while I sat in wonder, in awe of him. When he told me it would be all right, I believed him. He didn't think Ben would be put away, not with my help. I believed him.

He showed me how to dance. I danced with him. You can believe someone who can teach you to dance like this, believe me. We danced together as the road-show crew erected the gantries round us, dancing to the sound of hammers and oaths, to the music of the wolf-whistling roadies. My feet were so often off the ground, I knew we'd be far better than merely okay. I believed in this. This was the very thing. This was everything.

'You are my honey-honeysuckle,' Lovely Leo sang out, spoiling the music of the spheres again and again. He was becoming a poorer and poorer accompanist, a better and better interrupter of the new rhythm of my life.

'Why can't he ever leave us alone?' I asked Jag, whispering into the live round warmth of his close ear.

'He can't,' he simply said. 'That's all.'

That's all he said.

***

I was supposed to be resting in my dressing room before the show. Everybody was supposed to be leaving me alone. I wished they wouldn't. Trying to relax was winding me up. A text came through from Bex:

'GOOD LUCK!!!'

But the telephone's beep had buzzed through my head, vibrating, blurring my eyesight. I picked up my mobile, dialling for Jag.

'Amy!'

'Jag!'

'You're supposed to be –'

'I know. I can't. Can't you come here?'

He paused, as if he'd gone away for a few moments, then came back. 'Stay there.'

In three minutes, three and a bit, he was with me. I was in his arms. Three and a bit minutes, I know, because I timed them. I counted the seconds gone, surprised by how much time between each one.

'I can't do this without you,' I said.

For a moment, for a terrible moment, he tensed, as if to pull away from me. He looked into my face, and I could see he was smiling. He was glad, happy with what I'd just said. 'You don't have to do any of it on your own,' he said. 'I'm here. I'm here,' he said, kissing me. 'I'm with you. Don't worry.'

He made me feel safe. Excited, too. He kissed me, plunging his fingers into my short hair. His arms were so strong – not big, but lean and muscular, as he must be all over.

The knock on the door halted us. We came apart with difficulty, as if our clothes were sticking together with new velcro. Lovely Leo came blustering in, seemingly unsurprised to see us together there. Everyone must know everything, I remember thinking. I couldn't do a thing – *we* couldn't do a thing without them all knowing. I was such public property.

'Five minutes, just,' Leo flapped at us. 'Amy Peppercorn! Look at your hair! Oh! Come here, come here. Let's see what we can do. Where's your spray, dear? Really, this is – really!'

With Jag and me laughing, Leo pretended to be more and more outraged, making us laugh louder still. He re-spiked my hair where Jag had finger-combed it, until my last five minutes with Jag were all used up and we were on our way backstage for the first set in the first gig of Little Amy Peppercorn's very first UK tour.

***

The support band had been and gone, warming up the audience for us, their applause still evident in a restless noise, the sound of many calls and stray claps and whistles and the excitement of laughter. My own excitement felt like laughter itself, like Jag's kiss still warm on my lips, like the size and sound of our audience, the shivering hum of the silent, waiting sound equipment. I was quivering, literally shaking with anticipation behind or below the scenes, no longer tired, but high on my own wonderful nervous system and the pump and rush of sheer adrenalin.

I was wearing a tasselled skirt and top – too small really, too skimpy. But all my stuff seemed to be like that. None of it covered me properly. Not that I minded.

We didn't announce anything – nothing to announce. The band, all the musicians were on stage. Leo was there somewhere, behind the keyboards. Spotlights were coming on, sweeping the stage, over the audience, leaving, going out, as if flying away into the eternal background. The crowd started to applaud, then shriek. Drums started to beat, one or two keyboard flourishes from, I supposed, Lovely Leo. The crowd sounded as if they were shifting, flowing on a current of excitement. I felt as if they were getting all their excitement from me. My mind was everywhere all at once. I couldn't keep still.

Then – BANG! – the explosion that began the set, the fire and the smoke that exploded the rest of us up through the stage, singing and dancing from the very first moment. The crowd bubbled over, arms in the air. A new song, never heard before, called *Proud*. They never heard it now, such was the noise they were creating against the sound of my song. It didn't matter. We danced, I sang, the backing singers with me. Jag was with me the whole time. I could see him. More than that, I could feel him. We were wonderful together. I could do this. This was a pure perfect high, with a new energy surging through me, lifting me higher than I could ever have imagined. From where I sailed, I could look down on the crowded arena to see myself singing and dancing, having the time of my life.

The time of my life. I loved this. The first number finished to the applause that had continued throughout, a deafening, heavenly sound I wanted to wallow in for the rest of my life. We went straight into the second song, *The Word on the Street*. Never had I enjoyed that song so much. The words I knew so well and disliked so much took on another significance entirely as we danced, Jag and me, wildly, almost out of our minds, as the audience surged forward, some trying to make it up on to the stage. The roadies were throwing them back at first, before Jag signalled to them to let some through. Soon the place was one wild storm of dance, stage and auditorium one thing, unseparated, too chaotic to control. We had to keep the song going while the roadies cleared some of the people from the stage. They went, diving, crowd-surfing across a sea of hands held high.

I held the hand of a girl who looked like me. In fact, she looked very like me. She was my height, my build. She was probably years younger than me, but was made up with a face like mine, my spiked hair on her head. I held her hand. We danced, like twins. I cared about her when I had to let her go. She flattered me, wanting to look like me. All my life it seemed I hadn't wanted to look as I did; now young people wanted to be just like me, as did this girl, whom I had to let go, worrying that she wouldn't be able to find her friends or her family or whoever had brought her here to see me.

From there, I could see so many people, so many girls looking at me with my hair on their heads, their eyes made up to look like mine. I loved them for their affection towards me. Jag looked at them, I knew. He looked at me. He could tell the difference. I loved him – I think I loved him – for *his* affection towards me.

We did all the songs from the new album. This was going to sell, I knew. The songs were good. McGregor and Fine seemed fine to me at that moment. They were still good. Ray Ray did the business, despite being – being Ray Ray. Dreadful affliction, being Ray. Ray do suffer. Poor Ray. X-rated Ray, filthy stuttering mouth, finger on the pulse. No heart. That's his trouble. No heart.

So unlike me.

I don't know where the time went, because it seemed no sooner had we started than we were drawing to the end, or what I thought was going to be the end. In the end, the crowd were left calling, calling for something. I could hear what they were calling for.

Jag ran up to me. 'Can you hear that?'

'Yes,' I said. I looked out over a sea of heads, hands waving. I felt a wave of emotion, of love.

'You can do it,' Jag assured me.

I looked at him. For a moment we almost forgot where we were, so overwhelmed were we in the emotion of that moment. I could feel that Jag was feeling what I was feeling: love. We almost – we very nearly came together for the kiss, for Jag's kiss on the stage in front of however many thousand people this place could hold.

But the thousands called to us through the moment of our near-kiss, calling for something I said I'd never do again. Jag, his expressive face fully sharing my own expression of flowing emotion, assured me again that I could do it. 'You'll be fine,' he said, his face so close to mine. 'Everything's different now. Nothing's the same.'

I looked at him long and hard. His look back at me, as certain as his kiss, confirmed the changes in everything.

The crowd my audience were calling to me, calling me to sing the song of Geoffrey Fryer for them. As I looked out over the heads and hands, Jag looked round and signalled, I think, to Leo. The lights started to go down, a spotlight coming on.

I turned, indicated the reverse. I waved my arms to bring on the house lights, to tone down the stage spotlights. I wanted the crowd to feel as one with me, as I felt with them. I came to the front of the stage. Everyone else had moved back. We all stood still, as if we'd rehearsed this moment. We hadn't, of course. I was never going to sing this song again.

Until now, that is. Until the audience, the however many thousand, fell silent with me, standing as still as I was. There were however many thousands of eyes looking at me. I looked back. However many there were, I'm sure I made contact. I'm sure I looked at everyone there – everyone. If you were there, I looked at you. I know I did.

Pulling the fixed mike from the headpiece I'd been wearing, I picked up one of the loose hand-mikes that were dotted along the front of the stage. I held it, breathed. However many thousand breaths were held, a moment, a moment. I chose my moment, lifting the hand-mike. A moment more. One more.

You would seize the day for me . . .

And a roar of applause – long, lasting for as long as I smiled, as long as I laughed, taking a bow, thankful for the appreciation. I felt overwhelmed with love, forever in love. I laughed, holding out my arms. Imagine, not even as tall as a collapsed mike-stand, holding up my little arms and a huge crowded auditorium full of people falls silent. Try to imagine the power, the sparks flying from my fingertips, the laser lights beaming from my eyes. Again:

You would seize the day for me . . .

But now my voice against nothing but the heaving silence of the place, this big voice of mine flying from little me to them.

Me, giving this to them, giving something back for the appreciation, the affection shown to me.

Keep the night away for me
Make the darkness light for me
The noble sun ignite for me,
If ever, if ever you were here.

I didn't cry. I felt, with every fibre of my being, feeling the words, for Geoff, yes, for everyone. I felt for us all. I felt for Geoff, for Beccs, for Ben. I felt for Jag. And I felt for myself.

And if ever you were here again
I'd never shed a tear again
Or make the sunrise mine alone
Or see a new sun shine alone,
If ever, if ever you were here.

As I sang, the lights were coming on. Not the house lights, but the lighters – little flares blinking on all over the auditorium as the house lights dimmed and a single spotlight picked me out.

But nothing is forever now I know
The sunrise and the day will go
As the sun will burn to death one day
To be with you where you have gone
Where suns and stars have never shone.

Now, by now, the dark space before me was alight with firefly flares, little ignitions of light, of life in the darkness. My song, that old song I knew so well, or thought I did, changed its shape, its very meaning again. The song was full of hope now, of light in the darkness where suns and stars have never shone but where people have, people like Geoff, and like these people gently waving sparks of real life back at me as I sang:

Oh, you would seize the day for me,
Keep fearful night away for me.

And as I sang, so did they, the sparks of life, of hope, singing with me, overwhelmingly, as I turned the mike to them. They sang:

Make the darkness light for me
The noble sun ignite for me
If ever you were here with me
Once more.

Once more I sang with them, the band behind me striking up, somehow, with the sound of bells ringing, of choirs of backing singers singing, all of us crying out against the darkness:

Just one more day to keep
As darkness makes its way to sleep.

Our voices elevating, the roof about to fly away into a night no longer dark for our flares, our sparks, our wonderful voices holding each single, most powerful note:

To know that you've been near again
I'd never, ever shed a tear again.

And stop. The last most wonderful, powerful note hanging in the air. We waited. The note diminished but the flares, the sparks, didn't, wouldn't, ever. We stood, everybody, waiting.

I moved. I applauded. Yes! We roared our appreciation. Jag came running up. I swear there were tears in his eyes. There were none in mine. Love only. Only love.

Thirteen

I loved the world. Everything was moving, was sheer energy, with me, my energy, in the middle, in the very epicentre.

Jag kissed me after the concert. I kissed him. Everybody kissed, offering congratulations. Lovely Leo was lovely, ec-static. 'My Lovely, you were wonderful. Wonderful. Simply, simply wonderful!'

Jag was wonderful. The dancers, singers, the musicians. The roadies were wonderful, collapsing the set round us as we celebrated. Ray Ray appeared, not quite wonderful but not quite his usual quagmire of anti-wonder. 'Good,' he said. 'Very good. We got it good. Leo, you get our girl back. To bed, you,' he said to me.

I looked at Jag. He, faintly, shrugged.

To bed? How could I, with so much unused energy running through my veins at the speed of light? I had so much in me, so much love like a tempest unabated, firing me to a fury of dancing and laughing and the desire to kiss Jag's kiss.

'Let's go out somewhere,' I suggested to Leo, as he had us driven, with driver and bulked-up minder, back to the hotel. 'Let's go dancing. Let's get Jag and go dancing. Why do we have to go back? I'm hungry. I'm thirsty. I need to do something. I'm not finished. Why am I staying at that hotel all by myself?'

'Lovely,' he said, 'you're the star. Get used to it. The rest of us aren't worth that,' and snapped his fingers. 'You are the star of the show. It all happens round you, Sweet. It's a lonely planet, believe me.'

So, lonely, but buzzing, wildly energised, I couldn't eat the food that was sent to my room. It was late in the evening but felt so early. I took a bath to relax me. Bouncing out of the bathroom with more unwelcome energy than ever, I sent Beccs a text message:

'I LOVE THE WORLD!!!'

Because I did, and everyone in it. I felt special. The world had made me special, almost as if everyone in it had come to such a unanimous decision. I texted Jag:

'KISS ME GOODNIGHT.'

Jag was helping me let the world make me this special. He was part of it, a big part. Without him, this wasn't happening. If only he were here now, I was thinking, thinking about Jag again, again. Still thinking about him, trying to eat some of the food Leo had had sent up for me. I couldn't eat, couldn't sleep. Jag was too clearly on my mind, my body and brain still electrically energised by the gig, the girl that looked like me, the crowd, the audience, my fans. Yes, that's what they were – fans. It would have been embarrassing to use that word before now. Now it was right, it fitted. I had fans. They crowded out the concert venue, cheering, clapping, hands above heads, lighters lit like firefly flares.

If only Jag could have been with me there and then, to share it all with me. I tried to suppose he was sharing it, wherever he was, in whatever poky hotel or guesthouse Ray had stuffed everyone else into. Jag was, surely, experiencing the same sentiments and emotions as me. He definitely was. I could feel it, even though his mobile was off, which might just mean that he was asleep. He wasn't asleep. Not Jag. He was awake, very much so, thinking about kissing me goodnight.

That's what I was thinking about. If he'd been with me there and then, we'd have kissed. How we would have kissed! I lay back on my big bed thinking of kissing Jag, thinking of what it would have been like being here with him, having him with me all night. Being with him, having him with me.

I sat up. The thought of – of all night. Jag with me. Sleeping with me. Sleeping with me?

'I NEED TO TALK TO YOU' I texted Bex.

I needed to tell her everything. Beccs would understand. She would be with me, telling me what to do. I just hoped she'd tell me to do what I wanted, because I now realised what I wanted, and wanted so very, very badly.

***

There was no sleep for me until the morning light of Manchester was being kept out by my thickest of thick hotel drapes. All night I'd been pacing the densest pile I'd seen in a carpet since my dad's choice for home, throwing myself on the bed and the settee periodically to fail once more to fall asleep.

So it was until Leo was knocking at my door, at which time, of course, I was sleeping just about the deepest sleep of my entire life. I had to quickly take a shower and grab a cup of tea, purposely forgetting to take my medication. Jag would see to that for me. I loved, I simply loved giving him the opportunity.

Then we were on our way to the next venue, which wasn't that far away, but far enough to give me time to ask Leo, as we both sat in the back of the car, if he'd ever been in love.

'Lovely,' he said, with his eyes as sparkly as his sweater, 'I'm always in love. I'm the original martyr to love, believe me,

Sweet. Love? Please don't talk to me about love. You'll have me gushing. Sometimes I think I hate love.'

I laughed. 'You can't hate love.'

'Can't I?'

'No. Love is to be loved, or it doesn't happen, surely.'

'Oh, Lovely, you're so young. Let me tell you something. Can I tell you a little secret? Girl talk?'

I laughed again. Talking to Leo was very like talking to a woman, an older sister perhaps, such was his peculiar understanding.

'Promise me you'll listen. Promise me?'

'I promise, Leo. You're lovely, do you know that?'

Leo tutted, raising his eyes to the roof of the car. 'Please, Sweet, be gentle. You don't know how many people I'd kill to have looks half as good as yours.'

'Mine?' I said, genuinely surprised.

'Cheekbones, Lovely. Lips. Eyes.'

'Height?' I said.

'Height? With your figure? Who needs it?'

I used to think I did, I was thinking.

Leo was still tutting. 'No, listen, Lovely. Girl talk. Are you listening? Promise? A girl's got to learn how not to love, do you understand? A boy, a man, men – they just choose not to if they don't want. But a girl? You have to learn how not to give. Can you even begin to understand me?'

'But I don't want not to give,' I said.

He was looking into my face a long, long time. The car turned a corner off the main road. 'Cheekbones,' Leo said, smiling again. 'Lips. Eyes. All you need is some sleep, Lovely.'

'I couldn't last night. Too excited.'

'You will. All you need. You look fabulous, *fabulous*. At my age, sleep ravages one so. Not sleeping ravages one even more. Impossible, at my age. Have fun, Sweet. That's the main thing. Have fun. Oh, look! Your name in lights. The young star.'

'Too young?' I said to Leo, as the car pulled up outside our next venue, where my name, not in lights, was written large on to the fascia of the big building.

'Oh,' Leo said, 'one can never be too young, Lovely. Believe me.'

Yes, I believed him. When I could understand what Leo was saying to me, I believed him. *One* can never be too young, can *one*?

'I'm not too young, am I?' I said to Jag, taking my epilepsy pills like a good girl.

Jag was older than me by a few years. At my age, those few years were a lot. Too much, maybe? I thought.

He kissed me goodnight, his kiss among the set being erected about our ears.

'You're just right for me,' he whispered, in a bit of a shout above the roadie clamour of hammer and spanner. He kissed me goodnight in the late morning amid the chaos which was the clanging crashing crunching of my nervous emotions in the roadie road-show. He kissed me passionately, in full view. No, I was not too young. We had no secret to keep in Jag's kiss, public property that we both were.

I called Beccs just after twelve, knowing that she'd be about to take lunch. 'I think I'm in love,' I said.

'What have you done?' she said urgently, as if she'd just been talking to her mother or mine.

'I've given a great first concert,' I said. 'It's like nothing I've ever done. Beccs, the people! Everything! I can't explain it. I do love the world.'

'And your dancer?'

'Yes – I don't know. How does anybody know?'

'You be careful,' she said. 'How does he feel about you?'

'He says I'm just right for him. Beccs, I think I am, too. I really think so. What shall I do?'

She laughed. It was so good to hear her. She was like me. We had secrets together, shared our lives. I missed her.

'I really miss you,' I said.

'I do you,' she said straight away, feeling like I did. She was like me and I was like her.

'He's beautiful, Beccs,' I said.

'I know he is,' she said.

'And he cares about me.'

'Does he? Are you sure?'

I tried to look over at Jag then, just to see him as I talked about him to Beccs. He wasn't there. Leo wasn't there.

'Be sure,' Beccs warned.

'Okay,' I said. 'But – what then? What when I am sure? What then?'

For a long time we didn't say anything. Then we suddenly laughed. We laughed and laughed.

'Listen,' Beccs said. 'Good news. Ben's mum says yes. She wants a good lawyer for Ben.'

'Good,' I said. 'I'll get my dad to arrange it. That's good.'

'And,' Beccs said, 'I don't know what you'll think of this. Mrs Fryer wants to see if you'll come back to do a proper memorial for Geoff. She said the school can do a charity thing, after the last one went so badly wrong. She wants me to let you know she doesn't think any of it was your fault. What do you think? You could do a song.'

'A song?'

'Yeah. Not *that* song. I know you wouldn't want to. But we could make it a celebration, couldn't we? It could be really good for everyone. Clear the air.'

'I'm on tour.'

'After that. When you get back. Mrs Fryer would really like us to do something. They could make the arrangements, Mrs Fryer and the school.'

'For charity? Selling tickets?'

'Why not?'

'I'll have to clear it with – you know, my manager. But I can't see any reason why not.'

I could, actually, as Ray Ray rolled into view, also on his mobile, laughing most dangerously, noticing me there on my mobile but pretending not to. 'Leo says at our age,' I said to Beccs, 'we've got to learn how not to love.' I was watching Raymond as his laughter bit lumps out of the air. 'There are too many people that know only too well how not to love, don't you think?'

'Who's Leo?' Beccs asked eagerly, forgetting that she'd met him. 'Is he another dancer? Is he good looking? Can't you get a good-looking dancer for me too?'

I called my dad. 'That's a cement mixer, that is,' he told me. 'Don't touch it!'

'I won't,' I said.

'No,' he said, 'George! Jo! Oh, go on then. A bit of cement never hurt anyone. Unless it's gone hard, of course. You'll buy them some new clothes, Ames, won't you?'

'How much money have I got left?' I said.

He laughed. 'Left? You've got about thirty-odd thousand more than last time you asked. It just isn't going down. You're loaded, Kid.'

Ray was still laughing. He was still pretending not to have noticed I was there. He looked like he was talking money, possibly with my dad.

'You there, Amy?' my dad said, proving the impossibility of his conversing with Ray at this moment.

'I'm here,' I said.

'How did it go? Last night? Good?'

'Good.'

'Good. We thought you were going to call this morning. You've missed your mum.'

'I was – up late. I couldn't sleep.'

'Too excited, I expect. Good though, was it? I bet it was. Ray told me it went well.'

I glanced up. Ray had disappeared.

'Yeah,' my dad went on. 'Knew it would. Had to be. Right for it. Dead right for it.'

I looked up again. It could have been that I was talking to Ray through the open gap of my dad's ear.

'Dead right, yeah?' he said, as Ray says. When Ray say, Dad jump, yeah?

'Yeah,' I said. 'Dead right.'

'Your mum will be sorry she missed you.'

'Will she?'

'Of course she will. Why are you asking like that? She misses you all the time.'

'I miss her, Dad. I really do.'

'You'll be home soon, won't you?' he said.

'Yes,' I said, although I meant I was missing her even when I was with her, as she never seemed to be with me. 'I'll be home soon – in a few weeks' time.'

'There you are then. No worries.'

'No worries, Dad?'

'No worries, Ames. You know me.'

Yes, I was thinking, I do. He was easy to know, very easy. My mother, however, was not.

'Are you sure Mum's all right, Dad?'

'What? Jo! Oh no! George! Amy! Got to – call me back. Oh, blimey! Look out! Not the – Bye, Ames!'

Parents, eh? They're a constant worry, even after they've grown up; which, in fact, they never seem to be.

I'd forgotten to tell my dad to arrange the lawyer for Ben, but the battery was going on my mobile now. I was going to have to borrow someone's charger. Over one side of the stage, Ray was about to join Leo and Jag for a cup of coffee. Ray was still smiling. None of them seemed to notice me as I looked for somewhere to plug myself in.

***

That night, first set, second gig, first Little Amy Peppercorn UK Tour, we actually managed to get some of the first song heard: my next single from the album. The album was going to be called *Proud*. This was going to be the title track:

Coming my way
See your face in the crowd
Every day
Hear them voice out loud
Hearing them say
You're so proud, so proud
Of the way you look
It shouldn't be allowed.

I don't care anyway
I'm proud too.
I want them all to hear me say
I'm proud of you.
Beauty's deep as only skin, they say
But I don't think that's true.

I feel your beauty through and through
They don't know you like I do.

They don't know you like I do.
They don't show through like you do
I'm proud of you.
I'm proud of you.

McGregor and Fine were putting words in my mouth, but I was letting them out again to give them to Jag. Every song sounded better, given the enthusiasm and the energy that Jag had given me. 'I'm proud of you,' I sang, dancing, giving everything to the song, the audience of my fans, giving to Jag. He gave too, giving back to me – our faces, our smiles reflected one against the other. Last night I'd had practically no quality sleep, except for the half-hour or so too late in the morning, but it didn't matter. Enthusiasm and energy seemed to be given me in a packet, as my epilepsy tablets were handed over. I took my medicine, finding it a very, very effective remedy. The sparks flew out of my fingertips again. I faced the crowd, the audience of fans, the girls who looked a lot like me, the boys with them, keen to be seen with someone that looked like me. Two songs into the set and I was flying on the wings of love, giving everything away as if I had the world in my grasp. Maybe I did. It felt like it. I had everything, or so it felt. I could give and give, still there was more. It was never-ending. I was the most generous person alive, more alive than anyone that had ever lived. I could fly, really fly. From one side of the stage to the other I went without touching the boards. I was great.

So was Jag. He was with me. His face, his eyes made contact. He wouldn't let me go. He'd never let me down. We communicated with a single look, saying all these things to each other, vowing to keep it special, as precious as this.

I did *If Ever* again at the end. It felt fresh, like a new song. The lighters glimmered our commitment to a future of hope as the words I'd sung only to Geoffrey Fryer were dedicated to us all. We were left in the world; Geoff wouldn't want us not to love it, I was sure.

For an encore we did the new song *Proud* again. We did the song proud, Jag and me, together making it exceptional, its words specific to our very special communication:

I feel your beauty through and through
They don't know you like I do.
They don't know you like I do.
They don't show through like you do
I'm proud of you.
I'm proud of you.

So proud, we felt, I could feel, that we were beginning to belong to each other. One day we would, we would have to belong one to the other entirely. I could feel it. I could feel Jag feeling it.

The end of the concert came. Nothing could stop this. We were too powerful. *I* was, but Jag was with me. We kissed.

We kissed. I thought I was going to explode. His lips, his face against my own, the unbearable touch of our skin together. I couldn't contain it. I was bubbling over. 'I think I –' I was trying to say, to express how I was feeling to Jag.

'I know,' he had to say, as so many people wanted a piece of what we had, so many very excited people to meet, pulling us apart. I had to do the rounds of the media types, the people from the local press, the local radio stations, the regional TV studios, the music press, all sorts of other hangers-on clutching at Ray Ray's coat-tails. Very soon, too soon, it was late and Leo was charged with ensuring my safety to the hotel. Not on his own, of course. Lovely Leo was afraid of the dark and everything that moved in it and everything that didn't. We were forever ferried, shepherded, driven by beefsteak bouncers in chauffeur or black suits and dark, reflective sunglasses. Leo was afraid of them too, which made him feel a whole lot safer.

Still, he was my lady-in-waiting, always unexpectedly at my side ready to inform me when it was time to leave. By Leo-time, I never wanted to go. I was too high. I felt too much. I wanted to drink something, to eat the world in great, greedy chunks. I wanted Jag. I wanted to be with him, to have him by me. He wanted the same thing, I could see. But neither of us could see across or through the dark expanse of the meathead drivers and their shotgun-riders. Leo had them lift me clear, whisking me away through lamplit backstreets that were still surprisingly crowded with young fans.

'There are so many young girls still out on the street,' I said. 'Look. So many.'

'Oh, don't tell me, Lovely,' Leo squirmed. 'I despair, absolutely despair. Where are their parents? That's what I'd like to know. I just thank my stars I'll never need worry about a daughter, that's all I can say. I have enough worrying about you, Sweet. Don't talk to me about all those others. I mean, give me a break. Don't I worry enough already?'

By now, I was laughing too much to try to stop Leo. Whenever he got going there was no stopping him, anyway.

'Ooh, I'll never be a hard-man,' he said, glancing at the meat-men in the front of the car. 'All those hours I've spent in the gym,' he wailed, 'and look at me! I have to envy the street sparrows their leg muscles. And my knees? I'm just a bundle of cracking sticks, that's all I am. Ooh, what I'd do to have a figure like yours!'

Someone, a young girl like me, ran out in front of the car. We had to pull up suddenly, which stopped Leo in full flight as he and I tumbled forward. The car quickly turned, went round the girl as she stood looking in at us. She could see me looking at her. I tried a wave, but I didn't know if she saw.

One of the two dark suits in front looked round at Leo as he adjusted his clothing, checking his hair, picking the stray bits from the sleeves of his sparkly woolly.

'She's still out,' I said.

'Yes,' Leo tutted. 'Don't we just know.'

'Leo, can't we go somewhere? I'm all keyed up. I can't – I don't want to go to any boring hotel. I want to dance, with Jag. Leo, why can't we?'

He was shaking his head all through everything I was saying. 'No can do,' he said, patting his thick curly hair as it tipped the sides of his neck. 'Look at the time, Sweet. You have to sleep. Big day tomorrow.'

'Big day every day,' I said.

'Every day, Sweet,' he said.

'Big days always end when I don't want them to.'

'They have to end.'

'But I can't sleep. I won't be able to tonight. I can feel it.'

'You have to sleep, Lovely. Or you'll be horrible, and everyone would hate you.'

'No, they wouldn't. Not everyone.'

'Nearly everyone.'

'Oh Leo, I'm just – it's – I can't keep –'

'Look, Lovely, if you can't sleep, I'll give you something to help.'

'Something?'

'A little . . . something. They always work. I use them all the time. Just let me know.'

'I don't want to take . . . something. Anything.'

'All right. But you must sleep. You must.'

'Is that an order?'

'Of course. Naturally.'

'From whom?'

'What?'

'From whom? Who gives the orders, Leo?'

'Oh, you know. God, I suppose. If you don't sleep, you get ugly. Believe me, I know.'

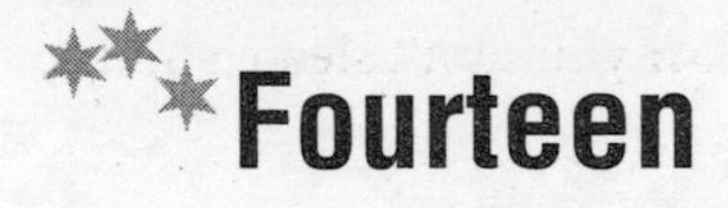

Fourteen

No sleep at all that night. I'd never gone a whole night without sleeping in my entire life. There just wasn't any to be had. Sleep had never felt so far away. I didn't feel tired. I got hungry, but not tired.

But then, in the back of the car on the longish drive up the motorway to the next city, it was lights out time. I couldn't even remember going off – I just stopped, maybe in mid-sentence. Maybe Leo was going on and on about something like an old or a too young woman, which was enough to send anybody to sleep. He was either one thing or the other, Leo – funny or a sure cure for insomnia. Whatever Leo was, he was still being it when I woke suddenly to find I'd been asleep, with Leo gassing on about colouring your hair and how grateful I should be that I didn't have to.

'What I'd do to have hair like yours,' Leo turned and said. 'Sleep, Sweet? Do you really want to make yourself ugly? Let me tell you, being ugly is the simplest thing in the world. Anyone can do it. Isn't that right, boys?' he said, cheekily directing his question towards the driver and his shotgun twin in the front of the car. The boys ignored Leo, as they did. The black suits hardly ever said anything at all, without ever seeming to notice that Leo existed.

'I'm tired,' I told Jag that morning, after he had kissed me goodnight. 'I'm not sleeping. Why can't I see you after the show?'

'We can't. Against the rules.'

'Whose rules?'

'You need your rest.'

'But I'm not sleeping. I want to see you. We – I need to talk – to be with you for a while. Let's just go, tonight.'

'Tonight?'

'After the show. Let's go dancing.'

'Dancing? I'm all danced out by then.'

'To a restaurant.'

'No. We'll be seen. There'll be a fuss.'

I stopped. My head was swimming.

'Look at you,' Jag said. 'Look, take your tablets. You'll be having a seizure at this rate if we're not careful.'

'Don't be careful with me, Jag,' I said. 'Be anything but careful. How do you feel about me?'

He stopped then. He looked at me. 'Don't you know?' he said.

From the way he was looking, I could tell, I could see, above all I could feel how he felt about me. We kissed. We felt the same about each other.

A hung-over roadie trailed cigarette smoke past us, as if we weren't there. I wished we weren't, that we were somewhere else, alone, for once.

'I need us to be together for a while,' I said.

'We will be,' he whispered, pressing the side of my face with his.

'Tonight,' I said.

'Yes,' he whispered. 'I need that, too.'

'Come to the hotel,' I said. 'Just for a while. I need to talk to you.'

'We need to talk,' he said.

'Will you, then? To the hotel?'

'Yes,' he said.

***

I texted Beccs:

'HE'S COMING TO MY ROOM. 2NITE.'

She called, immediately. Good old Beccs.

'Your dad hasn't contacted Mrs Fryer about the solicitor,' she said.

I stalled. I'd forgotten. 'He's forgotten,' I said. 'He's useless. I'll call him. He's useless.'

'It's all on, anyway,' she said. 'The concert.'

'Concert?'

'The charity concert. For Geoff. It's – everyone's really excited. Mrs Fryer wants it to happen. After your tour. Kirsty's having nothing to do with it. She's been hanging round with Sara Johnson quite a bit. Sara's like her. I don't care.'

'Didn't you get my message?' I said.

'Message?'

'Text?'

'When? Wait a minute – coming through now. What's it say?' Her mobile started to beep into my ear as she went into her messages. 'Oh my God! Amy! Oh no! What are you going to do?'

I laughed.

'Listen,' she said, 'sorry. There was me going on and on about Kirsty and Sara and all that little stuff I'm involved in. There's you –'

'No, Beccs. Don't. It's important, what you do.'

'I'm playing footie this afternoon,' she said.

'Are you? Beccs, that's great. You're good.'

'I know,' she laughed. 'I am. I love it.' She was just like her old self, bubbling over with the things she was enthusiastic about. 'You're my best friend,' she suddenly said, a few of her bubbles popping, too many others going flat.

I didn't like the way she sounded. As soon as she told me I was her best friend, I could hear further than the froth of her forced enthusiasm, all the way to her hidden loneliness and her hurt at having been deserted by her best friend and then her best first cousin. 'We'll always be friends, Beccs. I'm glad you're playing football. It suits you.'

'Yeah, I know.'

'Now,' I said, 'tell me about school and everything. Tell me about Mrs Fryer,' wanting not to bombard my friend with any more of my self-obsession, as I had, I realised, fallen into the habit of doing. I wanted to hear about Beccs, rather than running through how fantastic it was to be me, on stage before however many thousands of my fans.

'No,' she said, 'it's nothing compared to what you're doing. Mrs Fryer's a lovely lady, but I don't want to talk about her. Or Ben. I want you to tell me about tonight. Your dancer. Tell me about Jag. And everything.'

So I told her about Jag. I told her how he made me feel. She felt for me, I knew.

'What are you going to do?' she asked.

'I'm going to sing,' I said. 'I'm going to dance. I'm going to love it, love it, love it! That's what I'm going to do.'

***

'No you are not!' Ray Ray raged, when I told him about the memorial, and the fact that it had been turned into another concert, another L.A.P. gig. 'No way! Not, no more! All that! It's over! Hear me? Professional or nothing. Hear me? Don't argue!'

Don't argue! Ray say. I pay. Every day I sing, I dance, I give, so much, so much. Ray take. Ray, the taker.

So I cried, I don't know why. I'd have just liked, just liked to have some control, some little tiny piece of control over my own life. Yes, control can come in pieces, as it can come *to* pieces into chaos. I knew about that. But surely I wasn't just one thing or the other? Surely my life wasn't simply Ray's rules or my own aimless bedlam, one thing or the other?

But see my chaos, the confusion I had to try to put right by phoning my dad urgently, to get him to make the arrangements for Ben's solicitor, for Ben's bail. That was little Amy Peppercorn making hurried arrangements through tiredness and emotional stress, expecting a little more support from other quarters than merely a watered-down version of Raymond Raymond.

'Well,' my dad said, when I cried, weeping for Geoff, for the fact that I was probably going to have to let him down once again, 'well, if Ray says no, there's not much you can – I mean, he's manager. He manages. Managers manage, yeah?'

'I need to talk to Mum,' I said.

'Call tonight, then,' he said. 'Oh, no, wait a minute. What is it tonight?'

'Is she still doing night classes?'

'She's gone back to them. All of them, I think. More, maybe. I don't know. I can't keep track. She can't relax, she says.'

Neither can I, I was thinking. I can't sleep. I need to go to relaxation classes with my mum. I need to do something with my mum. Something. Anything.

How could I tell Beccs, now, that I couldn't do the memorial for Geoff? I wasn't allowed. The big pop star, not allowed to do what I wanted for one evening. Even for the smallest part of one evening.

'I really must see you tonight,' I had to go to Jag to confirm. 'You will be there, won't you?'

'What's wrong?' he said, with such caring in his face,

anybody could have seen it. Everybody did, everybody within eyeshot of where we were standing. Leo saw it. He watched us. He saw everything.

'I'm feeling so – I'm feeling – so cut off. I'm isolated. There's nobody to – to –'

'Come here,' Jag said, as Leo looked away. He held me tightly. I clung to him so hard. I'd never held anybody so hard in all my life. 'Hold me as tight as you like,' Jag whispered. 'As tight as you like.'

A little gasp came out of him as I held tighter, still tighter, squeezing out the energy and enthusiasm I needed but didn't have without him.

Fifteen

I wanted to do *Proud* again, at the very end of that evening's concert. We'd done it at the beginning, as usual, but it wasn't until the end that I really felt for it. The excitement, the elation wasn't really happening for me. I don't know if it showed in my performance. I hope not. Jag knew though. He kept coming to me, dancing out of turn, changing things so that the other dancers had to improvise to keep up. They liked it that way. So did we.

It worked. Jag worked his magic. I came alive. I started to feel the clothes I was wearing, the trousers slitted at the sides, the wonderful little short silver top. I could feel the changes in me like a change of clothes. It was as if Jag was replacing my blood, throwing out the old thick, sluggish stuff, replacing it with the good, the electric blood with sparks of fire in it. This is the stuff on which I can fly, because I *can* fly. I've had so many dreams where I can just, by sheer act of will, lift myself off the ground, float to the top of the room, hover around looking down on to the heads of the people underneath me. Well, on stage, with the electric blood flooding through me, that is what I can do. I can fly! I *can* fly! I did Jag *Proud*. There was something so extra-special about tonight, as my blood came up and my sense of worried isolation disappeared as far into the background as it could go. It didn't go away – it had been with me ever since I had learned of the car crash in which Geoff had died – but it had to glower on the other side, deep into the other half of me that had become subdued by the massive outpouring of the love I loved to feel on stage.

All the people I met after each concert were there to feel, to catch, to try to keep for themselves some of the excitement that flew from me into the world. They couldn't keep it – they didn't love enough.

I did. I loved so much, so hard, so wildly, my love sparked into the air, trying to teach ten thousand stars to dance, as Jag had taught me. Behind it all, then, him. Jag. They don't show through like you do. I'm proud of you.

I'm proud of you.

***

'You're crazy, do you know that?' Lovely Leo was saying as we were being driven to the next hotel.

Hotels, already, were beginning to look all the same. The rooms were sometimes a different shape, some with a different picture above the bed, but not often. Mostly they were copies of the same catalogue photograph, with free shampoo and shower gel that smelled too strongly of raspberry or deep peach.

Tonight, though, I couldn't wait to get there, wherever it was. I can't be too sure about where we were, exactly; it didn't matter. This room, tonight's similar version, Jag would be coming to when Leo and the big boy drivers were safely asleep or guzzling beer in the bar, according to their preference.

'I love you!' I was insisting to Leo.

'You're crazy. Crazy and lovely.'

'And I love you too,' I told the bare-knuckles in the front, who both pretended not to hear through the glass dividing the driving section from the back of the limo.

'Really!' Lovely Leo pouted, doing his mock-shock impersonation. 'Methinks the lady loves too much.'

'You can't love too much,' I said. 'You can't possibly,' with love sprouting from my fingertips like longer, lovelier nails. 'I can feel love with my hair,' I said.

'Oh,' Leo sang, *'I like women like women like men, so why don't women like me?'*

I laughed all the way to the hotel, with Leo singing his songs and flinging his arms, while the front boys frowned and scowled at everyone and everything.

***

Jag felt great too. He showed me how he felt, again and again, as soon as he appeared in the doorway of my hotel room.

'I'm proud of you,' he said.

I flung myself into his arms. He kissed me. So wonderful. He had to manoeuvre us into the room to close the door.

'I'm so glad you came,' I said. 'I'm proud of you.'

'I'm proud of you, too,' he said.

We kissed. We kissed, kissed. I can't tell you how wonderful it was to have Jag in my arms. Shivers were running all over me. I didn't know where I was, or, really, what I was doing. All the worries I had over my family and my few friends had evaporated. They didn't exist. For the moment, for the series of beautiful moments, I was just this: Jag's kiss.

'There's so much I want to say,' I said between kisses.

'And me,' he said. 'You're fantastic.'

'So are you.'

'On stage,' he said, 'it's like – like –'

'Like flying?' I said.

'Yes,' he said, with all my own enthusiasm, all my familiar

passion, 'yes, like flying. I've never known anything like it. It couldn't happen with anybody else. I know that.'

I knew it too. Not with anybody else. For Jag it was with me, for me with him. Everything felt right for us.

'You haven't eaten,' he said, noticing my untouched plates. 'Amy, you must eat regularly. What have I told you?'

'I couldn't,' I said. 'Don't tell me off.'

'I will tell you off,' he said, holding me tighter, 'if you don't look after yourself properly.'

He held me. It was such a moment of tenderness and care I could feel the tears welling up in me. I choked back a cry.

Feeling it, Jag moved me so that he could look into my face. 'Tears?' he said, touching one from my cheek. 'You look so lovely when you cry.'

'I'm not crying,' I said. 'I'm laughing really. I'm loving this. I *need* this. I *need* you, do you know that?'

He brushed another tear from my face.

'Don't go away,' I said.

'I'm not going to,' he said.

'No,' I said. 'I mean tonight. Don't leave me tonight.'

'You want me to stay here?'

'I want you to stay.'

We were whispering. This was secret.

'I think I love you,' I said.

He looked all over my face. My mascara was probably running. I didn't care. He could see me, whatever.

'I think I love you,' I whispered again.

'And I'm the same as you,' he whispered, looking at me, deeply into me.

'Are you, Jag?'

'Yes, I am. We're the same, Amy. We feel the same.'

'Then – you think you love me?'

'We're the same. We're flying, aren't we? Flying over everything? Yes, we are. But we need to be sure, though, about each other, don't we?'

'How can we be? How can you be sure?'

'Amy, listen. I'd love to stay with you tonight. I'd love to, but –'

He faltered. 'But?' I said. 'You have some buts about it?'

'So do you,' he said. 'We need to be sure. No one can be sure, absolutely, but – I can't just – not if it might not be right.'

'I can't stand it the way it is, Jag. I can't get near enough to you, or anyone. I'm flying half the time, the other half – I'm on my own. I'm lonely, Jag.'

'Don't be, Amy. Don't be. I *do* care. That's why I'm not going to stay tonight. If I didn't care, I just wouldn't care. I do, Amy. I can't tell you how much. Now I need to get you to eat something.'

'I don't want to. I'm not hungry.'

'It doesn't matter. You must eat regularly. You know the rules.'

'Rules? Everyone's always going on about rules. Who makes the rules? That's what I'd like to know.'

'Amy, chill. After the tour –'

'After the tour? Nothing changes. I told Beccs I'd do a thing for our friend that got killed in that accident –'

'Geoff?'

'Yeah. They want me to do a memorial concert for charity.'

'Who does?'

'Geoff's mum. My old school. Beccs does. That's the important thing. Beccs wants me to.'

'Then do.'

'Oh. Just like that? When Raymond makes his mind up as he goes along –'

'Ray?'

'He won't let me do it.'

'Why?'

'I don't know. Ask him. See where it gets you.'

'Forget it,' Jag said. 'Forget him. Do the thing for Geoff. I'll find a way round Ray.'

'Are there any ways round Ray?'

'I'll tell you something about Ray,' he said, 'shall I? It's all in the approach. You get the right angle, you get what you want.'

'I don't know the angles,' I said.

'No,' he said, 'but I do. So eat your dinner and don't worry about it. Tell Beccs yes. You need to sleep – look at you. Here, let me give you a kiss goodnight.'

'You're not going already, are you?'

'No. I want to make up for all those kisses goodnight I've had to give you in the morning. This is the first kiss goodnight I've given you at night. This is the second. This the third. It won't be the last.'

'I don't want there to be a last.'

'There won't be, don't worry. There won't be.'

***

I'd had to go and ask Leo to get me those little somethings to help me sleep. He dipped into his pocket there and then, on the way back from the gig, whipping out a little plastic pot of pills. 'One a night only,' he said.

'What are they?'

'Lovely, they're all natural. They're herbal.'

'They don't look it,' I said, having flipped the lid, looking down into the vial at the cluster of white tablets.

'Sweet, tell me, what did you expect? Moss? Some kind of rain-forest vine? They're made from herbal ingredients. If you put one under your tongue, your tongue will go numb. Take one, you'll sleep. I promise you.'

I had to have one after Jag left, having had practically no sleep again the night before. My mind, my muscular brain never knew when to give in. Jag was imprinted there – everything he said went winding through my mind on permanent replay. He had kissed me goodnight in bed – with me in bed. He'd waited while I took off my make-up, cleaned my teeth. I'd felt so nervous of him seeing me. I'd started wearing this little pants and vest outfit for bed. I was supposed to wear it on stage, but it was just too tiny and too flimsy. But it was Jag seeing me without make-up that I was most nervous about. If he still likes me after this, I was thinking, there's nothing I can't face with him.

He watched me as I emerged from the bathroom wearing what I was wearing. He was standing there – combats, vest, skin, beauty. I felt quite plain, more ordinary, but it thrilled me to have him look at me in that way.

Jag pulled back the sheets for me. He helped me into bed. It was a moment of utmost tenderness. The way he left me, turning out the light as if I'd be able to sleep. I wanted to, without one of Leo's pills, but sleep wouldn't come. I tried without it. Jag's kindness, intended to help me, stopped me. He was still there with me, still too close, with his eyes on me as I emerged from the bathroom feeling with every nerve-end every movement of my body under his gaze. It was wonderful, being looked at like that. So warm. So right. Yes, it was right. I already knew. I'd made up my mind. It was wonderful of Jag to want to wait until the end of the tour, and I loved him for it. But I didn't need any more convincing than the fact that he had chosen to wait – that, and how it felt when he looked at me. It must be difficult to know, to *really* know when you're in love, but feeling like this when looked at like that – it must be a part of it. A very big part of it. In fact, as I lay there trying to resist one of Leo's tablets, I couldn't think of what else there was to consider. I felt like this. If he felt the same, as he did, that was all there was to it, wasn't it?

In the end, having re-lived every moment of my first real evening with Jag through and through, I took the pill, holding it under my numbing tongue, expecting to be knocked senseless on the instant. Nothing happened. My mind kept going and going. My tongue was fast asleep, but nothing else was. The night went on and on with my infinite brain on endless replay.

Sixteen

An unexpectedly strong burst of sunlight seemed to set my bedside telephone ringing like crazy.

'Come on, Lovely,' Leo was crowing, 'let's be having you. What were you doing?'

'Sleeping,' I moaned.

'Sleeping!' he shrieked. 'Aren't you ready, Sweet? Really! We've got a long way to go today. Come on. Breakfast! I'll fetch it up. Shower! Quickly!'

'What have you been doing?' he flapped, when I opened the door in my bathrobe. 'Did you take one? Sooner, Sweet, rather than later. Look at you. Are you awake?'

I wasn't, not fully. Something about those little somethings to make me sleep made me want to sleep when I wanted to feel fully awake. I kept having to nudge myself into moving, into drying my hair, applying some make-up.

'My Sweet,' Leo spouted, 'you'll have to learn to get a pattern on tour. A rhythm, yes? You have rhythm, don't you?'

To be honest, I didn't know if I had rhythm ever, or what I had, if anything. There was no energy in my limbs. My head was full of cotton wool. I slept on and off in the car, which was not unusual, but couldn't shake off the feeling of sedation, this lacklustre lethargy that wouldn't let me move freely. It certainly wouldn't allow me to dance with Jag before the show, as we did, constantly, showing off more than rehearsing.

'What's the matter, Amy?' Jag had to come back and ask, having left me far behind on one side of the stage. 'You aren't with it today. Didn't you sleep?'

'I took a tablet,' I said. 'Leo gave them to me. I had to take one. I haven't slept at all. I can't. I need you with me.'

'Would you sleep if I was there?'

'I don't know. But it wouldn't matter then. I'd have you with me.'

Jag hugged me. 'Well, good morning,' he said, kissing me, although it was well into the afternoon by this time.

We'd just found out that *If Ever* had been surprisingly knocked off the Number One spot by a new single from Courtney Schaeffer. The papers were full of the feud between us, reporting on what I was supposed to have said about her, and she of me. They said that I'd said I didn't like what she'd done. It sounded as if I was talking about her knocking me from Number One, but it was, in fact, an old quote – my response to what she was supposed to have said about me in the beginning. The papers were so good, *so* good at bringing up something you once said and using it out of context. They can make you say things you never said about things you care so very little about.

All the road crew were going about saying what a bitch Courtney was. Leo despised her with such a passion, I couldn't help but suspect him of really liking her. I kind of liked her myself. I was pretty sure she was in the same boat as me, the two of us bobbing about on the tide, trying to do our best, getting carried away by forces beyond our control. So many other people depended upon our success. It wasn't easy.

Courtney was a bit older than me. She'd been around in the business that much longer. I found I wanted to ask her how she managed to rest, how she found the energy to do what she did for as long as she'd been doing it. She was my enemy in the press; privately, I felt an affinity with her, as if she might have known what I was going through.

'Let me know,' Jag said, drawing me to one side of the stage, 'how you feel a bit later on. If you're still tired, I can maybe help you.'

I trusted him. If Jag said he could help, then I was sure he could.

***

I called Beccs when I thought she'd be on her break at school. 'Good news,' I said as soon as she answered. 'I can do the memorial for Geoff. No problem.'

'I know,' she said.

'You know?'

'Your people have been on. They want a proper venue. It's going to be tagged on to the end of your tour. A few days after your last gig.'

'Oh,' I said.

'Have you seen the papers?' she said. 'Have you seen what Courtney's been saying about you now? When's your album coming out? The new single will soon knock her for six. *Proud* is a great song.'

'But – how –' I stammered.

'Raymond Raymond gave me a copy,' she said. 'The album and everything. I think it's great, Amy, I really do.'

***

'All in the approach,' Jag said, when I went back to him. 'Give Raymond something, let him get something out of it, you get what you want.'

'But it was supposed to be just a small thing, a school thing, and Geoff's mum and –'

'They're thrilled, don't worry. Everyone's pleased. See? There's a way round, always.'

'But it'll just be another gig.'

'No, it won't. It'll be for Geoff. His mum's doing something in the programme. All the money's going to charity. It'll be for Geoff. Open-air venue. Huge. Courtney'll be so jealous – what's wrong?'

'I don't – it wasn't supposed to be like that.'

'It's better, Amy.'

'And it won't leave us any time – we were supposed to be – after the tour –'

He smiled. He held me. I felt I could have fallen asleep against his chest, standing against him to one side of the stage. A strange dizziness overcame me, a weakness that was deeply within me rather than any encroaching epileptic electric gloom.

'After the tour,' Jag whispered, 'there's time for you and me.'

I looked into his face. He was taking note of my tiredness, my pale lack of energy.

'I'm seeing to it,' Jag told me, intimately. 'Time for us, with no one else there. If that's what you want?'

'That's what I want,' I said.

'Don't say anything to anybody,' he said. 'We'll get away. Leave it to me.'

He kissed me. I could have slept. It would have been beautiful, delicious, to have slept with him then, in his arms.

From one of the big pockets in his combats he produced a little container, not unlike the pillbox that Leo had given me. 'What's this?' I said.

He flipped the lid, glancing round. 'Take one,' he said. 'It'll perk you up.'

'What is it?'

'It's just – vitamins. I take them. Look, take one each. It's in addition to your medication.'

'Vitamins?'

'Multi-vits and minerals. You're run down. One of these will pick you up, I promise. Trust me.'

Seventeen

I could feel my heart going before the show. Jag gave me water. 'Drink lots,' he said.

I drank. We waited to go on. I'd spent the rest of the afternoon watching the roadies working. I knew some of them now, although they were very difficult to know. They were, most of them, so self-contained – just working and drinking coke and coffee and smoking cigarettes and eating about every hour on the hour. I'd never thought about it before, but they never seemed to sleep. There was I, lounging in a daze just watching these work-maniacs running through their clockwork paces. I'd be resting, trying to, in my plush hotel room, these guys would be dismantling the set, loading it all back on to the trucks, trucking it to the next town, the next city. There was no stopping them.

As I watched them, I seemed to be becoming infected by the roadies' energy. I could feel a kind of need to flex my hands and forearms. It made me feel like lifting some of the gear on to the gantries, some of the big black boxes that looked so heavy and must have done something crucial, although, of course, I had absolutely no idea what that something might have been.

We were pretty well prepared for the show when Jag stepped up to find out how I was doing. My heart was going. It always did, just before going on, sometimes sickeningly so; but this time it was different. The energy level, the energy itself was different, more intense at so early a stage, coming at me, rather than me drawing on it.

'Drink lots,' Jag said.

I had to. The weather was very warm. I was even warmer in my shorts and shimmering boots and top. We stood beneath the stage on the little round platforms that would elevate us quickly through the bottom of the stage, as if we'd appeared in the explosion and the smoke that announced our arrival. I was in the front, Jag and the other dancers behind. We waited. I couldn't wait, but had to. My blood was up for no apparent reason. I was juddering, pulsing with energy and the enthusiasm to go. We waited for the explosion for what seemed like a long, long time. I thought I was going to blow up.

I thought I was going to blow up, when BANG!

We shot through the stage into the rapture of applause and launched straight into *Proud*. I was proud, I don't mind telling you. It's essential, that pride, when you're on stage in front of so many. You have to have the pride it takes to do what you do, which is the thing that's brought so many here in the first place.

From the word go, from the explosion of our first appearance, my feet hardly touched the ground. Jag's multivits and mins certainly seemed to have done the trick. This was better than ever. My head knew what to do, was aware of what was happening, while my body flew free, as if my backbone wasn't there any longer. As if there were no longer any physical restrictions to prevent me from doing anything, anything at all. I was so powerful. Dancing came to me, to collect me. I didn't have to do a thing. The electrical energy of the storm clouds brewing outside fed their power straight into me.

I screamed at the crowd: 'Can you all hear me at the back? Can you hear me?'

They cheered and clapped their approval. This was the first time I'd addressed the audience like this, in spoken words, conversing with them.

'Are you having fun?'

They cheered. They were one voice, one fantastic universal voice calling back at me, responding to everything I had to say.

'I hope you're having a fantastic time,' I yelled into the mike. 'Listen,' I yelled, 'don't go home tonight. Stay here. We'll dance all night, yeah?'

A great cheer went up. The excitement bristled across my skin. 'Stay with me!' I screamed. 'Stay with me!'

The musicians were standing up behind me, applauding. Jag and the dancers were clapping with their hands above their heads.

'Stay with me! We're gonna go for it! Shall we go for it?'

The crowd cheered.

'I can't hear you!' I screamed all the louder. 'I can't hear you! Shall we go for it?'

The crowd responded. The noise was almost deafening.

'Go for it!' I screamed. They went mad. 'Go for it! What are we gonna do?'

They were with me, every single one – thousands, with no one, absolutely no one left out. Everyone was there.

'What are we gonna do?'

I held out a mike. 'Go for it!' the crowd bellowed back at me.

'I can't hear you! What are we gonna do?'

'Go for it!'

'Go for it!' I screamed back at them. 'Go for it!'

The noise was going to break down the walls of the place. I don't know where we were, I'd already given up trying to remember, but they'll remember us, wherever it was. At the height of the commotion the stage manager produced a piece of inspired theatre by exploding another row of flash-fire-bombs along the front of the stage. They'd normally have been used towards the end of the show, but we'd reached such a peak of excitement and noise level, some kind of explosion had to happen.

We exploded into the next number – drums, me, Jag and the dancers jumping through the smoke into the new spot-lights as if this had been rehearsed a thousand times. It hadn't. Nobody knew what I was likely to do next. I never knew. The road crew were brilliant technicians, so know-ledgeable and professional. I screamed out of turn, they turned it into an important part of the show. We were good, and getting better all the time.

***

'You're fantastic!' Jag yelled at me through the applause following our second encore. He gave me more water.

***

'Take one of those pills sooner,' Lovely Leo said, after having swooned in admiration for what we'd done on stage, 'rather than later. You're going to need to sleep tonight, Sweet. Come on, let me see you take it.'

***

'Mum!' I cried, yelling into my mobile as people partied all round me, drinking and laughing and generally showing off after the show. 'Mum! It's great to hear you. What?' I had to press a finger into my other ear to hear what she was saying.

'Mum, it's lovely to hear you. What? Yes, yes. We've just given a great show. Great show! What? Hold on, let me find somewhere quieter.'

Jamming myself into a corner, huddled over, I protected my mobile. 'Mum? Can you hear me? Don't go away,' I said.

'Away?' she said. 'Don't be silly. I'm here. How are you?'

'I've given myself a headache.'

'Be careful. You'll get a seizure.'

'No I won't. We've got all that sorted.'

'Oh,' she said. 'We have, have we?'

'Yes,' I said. There was a pause between us.

'You're looking after yourself, then?' she said.

Jag flashed through my mind. I felt like telling her that someone, someone special was looking after me, so no need to worry. All I said was, 'Yes.'

'How long have you got to go?' she asked, as if she didn't know.

'Just under three weeks. I'll be glad to be – at the end of the tour. It's hard work. I've missed you so much.'

'Yes,' she said. 'I've missed you. I want to see you, but I can't.'

'It'll all be over soon, Mum,' I said.

'Will it?' she said.

I looked over at Jag, for the support I needed against the loneliness I felt by being isolated from my family. He was talking to Leo. Leo glanced over at me. I could see it was nearly time to go. I could feel the numbness of Leo's sleeping pill at the back of my throat, prickling at my nose and the corners of my eyes, like a cold, or something even more dreadful coming.

'Will it?' my mum said.

Eighteen

All the while, Jag. From there on, through the low, high, low, every day, him. He kept me focussed – on wanting him, on wanting the end of a very successful first tour.

I was conversing with the crowd more and more as we went on, picking them up, playing them, bringing them on. The atmosphere of each gig told me what to say and do. I was right every time. The reviews in all the papers agreed:

'Little Amy Larges It Live!'

'Peppercorn Pumping!'

'Little Amy Peppercorn – Crowd Control!'

Always the exclamation mark at the end, the press seal of approval. And always, somewhere further down, a report on Courtney Schaeffer's dislike of my success, followed by an out-of-context retort from me.

I didn't mind. I didn't mind the numb tiredness of Lovely Leo's pills, as long as I slept and dreamt of Jag. I waited for the goodnight kiss throughout the following afternoons, for the multi-vitamined high of the next gig in the train of events that would lead me to the end and to my time with Jag.

You see, I loved him. If you don't know whether or not you love someone, you don't. I knew now. He was never really out of my thoughts. He was there inside every emotion; every sleeping, waking, conscious or unconscious feeling, he was.

We did the big universities, the concert halls, exhibition centres, a warehouse once, like a rave. In a little over five weeks I travelled most of the country – England, Wales, Scotland, seeing practically none of it. One place seemed so very like the next. The venues changed, the set didn't. My experience grew. I talked to the girls, my sisters, over the phone, as they yelled over my songs at me. My dad raved about money: Ben's solicitors were costing more than he could earn in a year. 'You can earn it in three days, though, Ames,' he said. My mum came on the phone and said very little. We were like strangers. Beccs told me how much Solar had included her and Mrs Fryer in the arrangements for the open-air concert for Geoff.

Through it all there was a loss of feeling for home for family and friends. Not a feeling of loss – a loss of feeling. The intensity of my passion for Jag got in the way, expelling everything else like a cuckoo in a wren's nest. He danced with me, kissing me good morning every night. He was beautiful. Everybody liked him, especially the girl dancers. I could see the way they looked at him. But then they looked at me with an unfriendly respect that managed to scare me slightly and satisfy me at the same time. They didn't seem to like me, in the way that girls don't like other girls. They wanted to take Jag away. Their faces told me that was what they wanted to do.

They couldn't. Jag was with me. He was mine. When their faces looked at him, they messaged availability, an approval. When his looked into mine, we were for each other. Ray Ray, silently watching, couldn't bring us apart. We were too together for them, enjoying ourselves with each other, waiting for the end of the tour when they couldn't watch us any longer.

***

'Ben's at home,' Beccs called to say.

'What? How?'

'Your solicitors,' she said. 'Yesterday, all of a sudden. Out on bail.'

'On bail!'

'A lot of money, Mrs Fryer said. You're putting the money up.'

'Am I? Mrs Fryer knows all this?'

'She's been helping Ben's mum. She doesn't want Ben put away. She's a lovely lady. You've done a good job, Amy,' Beccs said.

A good job? Mrs Fryer's dignified and noble behaviour, and my money! The grief of a mother and the wealth of a pop star? That such a woman should have been denied her son, that such a woman's son should have been denied! I wanted my own mother, my mum to be half as proud of my life as Mrs Fryer was of Geoff's.

I tried calling my mum that evening. She was at one or the other of her classes. 'She's hardly ever here nowadays,' my dad said. 'Anyway,' he bounced back, 'how's – where are you?'

'I don't know,' I said, calling to a beer-bottle roadie, 'Where are we? Leeds,' I said to my dad.

'Leeds! You're everywhere, Amy, aren't you? You're all over the place.'

I was, all over the place. Jag came by. I latched on to him. Without him, totally all over the place. 'I want you,' I said. 'I only want you. That's all. I don't know if I'm any good without you.'

'You're good,' he said. 'Don't worry. A couple more nights, then it's the last. Thursday, it's Bristol. The end.'

'Not the end,' I said.

'No,' he agreed, 'not that. Definitely not that.'

Nineteen

Our last gig of the tour: Little Amy was going large in Bristol. This was it, the end. The beginning.

'Hello, Bristol!' I yelled. The crowd were with me, whistling, calling, clapping. 'This is our last night!' I bellowed. 'You're our last gig! And you know what?'

Some responded. It's difficult to ask a question of a crowd and get a response. I did it. 'You know what?' I shouted louder, leaning dangerously over the front of the stage, running the full length and back. 'You know what?'

The crowd responded. They shouted back, screaming, applauding. I held them in my hands. My power was overwhelming, surprising everyone, including me. I was never this confident when I was being just me, painfully small Amy, worrying about what every individual thought of me whenever I had to speak to anyone personally. Like this, controlling a whole crowd, the power of my personality was redefined, taken away from the concerns that narrowed and confined me. On stage I was larger than life – much larger, obviously. Everything was so simplified whenever I was furious in full flight on stage, sheer and pure professional performer, giving myself wholly, receiving a crowd's communication in return. It was just like being in love. For me, that's what it was. Jag was going to allow me to continue to be this simply defined, to be this perfect on and off stage tonight, all night.

I didn't know where we were going. Jag told me only that everything was arranged. I was supposed to be going back to my hotel, alone for one more night before home tomorrow. 'You're not doing that,' Jag told me. 'We're doing something else, together. Don't say anything to anyone. I've got it all arranged.'

I didn't say anything to anyone, but shouted out my delight to my delighted audience on the last gig of the tour. 'Bristol! I love you!'

They loved me too. We went into *Proud*, having introduced it as the new single from the new album. 'I hope you've heard it,' I shouted out. 'Have you heard it?'

Their appreciation told me yes, they'd heard it, even those that were only pretending they had. But they probably had, we were getting so much pre-release radio play.

No one knows you like I do
No one shows through like you do
I'm proud of you.
I'm proud of you.

Yes, with the repetition of that last line they told me again that yes, they had heard and liked the song.

'I'm proud of you,' I sang.

'I'm proud of you,' they sang back.

It was fantastic. I did it again, holding one of the hand-mikes: 'I'm proud of you!'

The return came on stronger, louder, more passionately real: 'I'm proud of you!'

Again: 'I'm proud of you!'

Holding the mike out to my audience, my fans: 'I'm proud of you!'

Me, again: 'I'm proud of you!'

Them, once more: 'I'm proud of you!'

I screamed. I really did. So much inside me, so much to let out, to get out in one go. So much love. I was bubbling over, living large, loving every second, every single soul I could see, which was a whole town, a city full of souls.

The Bristol concert hall was alight with the hysterical flicker of camera flash before we settled into the anthem that *If Ever* had become. The flashgun tremor of cameras fell away into the soft candle glimmer of lasting light, the fireflies of hope glowing in the crowded darkness:

Just one more day to keep
As darkness makes its way to sleep
To know that you've been near again
I'd never, ever shed a tear again.

I swear I could feel the individual presence of everyone there that night. In accepting me, collecting every gift I had to offer, they communicated with me as I did with them, on what felt like a one-to-one basis. It was beautiful. We were alive. There was so much to be young for. This moment was worthy of our youth, our anxiety and uncertainty about our futures. This moment overcame all that, being for us the moment that we were, in which we were all right, doing good, living it.

A party was going on behind the set. Everyone was drinking and laughing. The press were there, all supplied with champagne, all quaffing it down. Lovely Leo was as sparkly as his sweater. Everyone was lovely, was a darling, a love. He was talking to everyone at once, to nobody in particular.

A glass of orange juice appeared in my hand just before someone topped it up with champagne. The press photographers snapped me up. I was laughing, loving too much, according to Leo, who laughed and loved too much himself, so what would he know?

Jag had disappeared. I didn't know what was going to happen next, but I hoped it would happen soon. The ladies and gentlemen of the press were being very nice, telling me how exciting the performance was. I was coming to recognise a couple of them. One said I was going from strength to strength. She'd seen me at the beginning of the tour, now at the end. 'You've learned a lot,' she said, smiling at me.

'I've learned how best to give,' I said.

'Ooh,' she said, writing it down, 'that was good. Can we get another photo?'

'What did you say to her?' another journalist sidled up and said.

'I said I've learned how best to give,' I said.

'Was that an exclusive?' he said.

I shook my head.

'Good,' he said. 'Can we get another photograph?'

'Take your tablet sooner rather than later,' Leo sidled up then. 'You'll need your sleep tonight. We'll want you looking lovely when we take you home tomorrow, won't we, Lovely?'

I put the pill in my pocket and looked about for Jag. He wasn't there. But not being able to see Jag didn't mean he wasn't with me. I could feel him. He wasn't far. I believed in him.

My belief wasn't to be disproven, either. Not there or then. The time came to leave. I left, walking in front of Leo as he kissed as many people goodbye as kissed me. The car drew up outside with our driver and my minder plumped in the front. Jag was nowhere to be seen, but he was close. My every emotion told me he wouldn't let me down.

I opened the back door of our limo. Jag hadn't let me

down. He dragged me into the back of the car, slamming and locking the doors before Leo could reach the handle. We laughed like crazy, both kneeling to look out of the back window at Lovely Leo doing a little harmless war-dance on the pavement outside the Bristol concert hall where Little Amy Peppercorn was written large above his cross curly head.

'Look at him!' Jag yelled. 'That's got rid of him for a while.'

We laughed and laughed. We kissed in the back of the car. We laughed some more. 'But how did you –' I said, through laughing tears of love.

'The guys are with me,' Jag said, nodding at the braves braced in the front of the car. Jag knocked on the glass separating us. The minder looked round. Jag gave him the thumbs up. 'Nice one, Steve,' he said.

I kissed Jag. I kissed him. This was the first time for weeks I'd been let off my leash. I felt wonderful. Everything felt continuously better and better. Surely this couldn't keep going, going from good to better to even better still until I went out of my mind with pleasure, could it?

'Where are we going?' I asked Jag.

'A long way. Somewhere nobody's going to be able to find us,' he said, touching my lips with his fingertip. 'Not until we want them to.'

'I might never want them to,' I said.

'Then we'll never go back,' Jag said, kissing me. 'We might never go back,' he whispered, his lips brushing warm against my ear.

I was going to go out of my mind with pleasure.

Twenty

We drove down to Cornwall. Just outside Newquay there's a big redbrick hotel that sits looking across the cliff-tops above the surf in the moonlight. We had a little balcony that allowed us to see for miles a moonlit coast so late at night when nothing's to be heard but the surf and our own hot bloodstreams. Jag's warm face pulsed against my own as he kept me warm in the chill not that long before the dawn.

We had driven all that way, but a night porter was waiting to receive us, unsurprised at our total absence of luggage. 'We'd like some toothbrushes and washing stuff,' Jag said to him.

'It's in your room,' he said.

Our room. *Our* room.

Minder Steve and the driver were losing the car; Jag and I were being shown our room. Jag tipped the night porter with a banknote that he pocketed without a second glance. Then he was gone.

The moon was up across the water outside our window like a pizza we'd ordered to go. We walked out, without saying anything, on to our little balcony above the white rim of waves that kept the sea from where we were staying. I shivered in the chill breeze. Jag held me.

'We might never go back,' he said.

We kissed.

I felt afraid. Suddenly too many things were whizzing

through my mind uninvited. My dad, his innocent trust apparent on his kind face. I shuddered away from the idea of my mum's eye, a sterner eye looking through my father's at his daughter. My sisters said 'Poo!' and held their noses. Geoffrey Fryer stuttered. Ben tried to kiss me in the hall at home, with my mum and dad arguing in the background.

'Keep me safe,' I whispered to Jag.

'I'll keep you safe,' he kissed me, cupping my face in his hands.

I held him. We stayed together, so close together without moving, planting ourselves into something longlasting, something permanent. We'd not be going back as we were. We were changing things here, permanently. In the stillness we could both feel the changes happening about us, with us, in us. Unmoving, we went about our changes together, of one mind. We were of one heart. I could feel, I could hear it beating.

'You're very special,' Jag whispered to me.

'So are you. Jag, keep me special.'

'I will. Always.'

'I don't know what to do now,' I had to say, because I knew we couldn't stay and starve to death; that we would have to go on living after the wonderful next stage of our lives. But how, I didn't have the experience to say. 'I don't know what to do,' I said. 'I mean, I don't know what I'm supposed to do next.'

Jag looked into my face. He smiled, not mocking, understanding. 'You stop worrying about it,' he said. 'That's what you do next.'

I smiled too. He gave me a little kiss on the mouth. So warm, even his little kisses, so intimate and soft.

'Look,' he said, going over to the bed. There were garments folded, one either side. He picked up a big red pyjama jacket.

We laughed. 'You want to use the bathroom?' he said.

I smiled; it was all I could do. Jag would make this easy, make this right for me. I picked up my bag, went into the bathroom.

***

Text:

'BEX, JAG & ME, 2NITE. WSH ME LUCK. SO SCARED! LV. A!'

***

I stood looking into the mirror in the bathroom, wearing only my little bedtime outfit. Jag had already seen me like this. I'd seen him occasionally with his shirt off. His body was beautiful – more lovely than mine, I thought. Looking into the mirror, I couldn't see anything but me, as I always looked, the same as every day. It didn't seem enough – not for Jag, the dancer, the Mystery.

He, when I saw him, was more beautiful, more mysterious than ever. He was wearing only the red silk bottoms from his side of the bed. He was standing waiting for me, with his slightly brown skin shining in the moon-like lamplight.

'You all right?' he said.

I nodded. I wasn't. My mouth was too dry. I couldn't speak. 'I –' I tried to say. 'A drink.'

Jag poured water from a little bottle from the drinks fridge in the room. I drank.

'Okay?' he said.

I nodded. I wasn't.

He kissed me. Our bodies touched. So warm. So warm, soft. Together. He held me.

'We've lots of time,' he whispered. 'The rest of our lives, if you like.'

I held on to him. He lifted me. My legs wrapped his waist. He was so strong, I was so light. I never knew I was this light. I must have weighed next to nothing. He could hold me. Everything I was, all that was me in worry, in fear and joy and love, he held. So simply. I loved the simplicity of being like this. How he made me feel. All that I had been afraid of, nervous about, went away. He held me off the ground, flying across the room like my dream, like on stage, for ages upon ages. We looked into each other. We kissed as he lowered me on to the bed.

He lay with me. 'Keep me safe, Jag,' I said. 'You know what to do, don't you?'

'I know what to do,' he said.

Twenty-one

The confusion of waking in a strange bed had disappeared long ago, after the first week or so of touring. But waking in a strange bed with the weight of someone sleeping beside me was very confusing.

There was a little damp patch on my pillow where I'd been dribbling. I lifted my head to look round at Jag. He was asleep, lying on his back. The quilt was pushed down to our waists. I had to just look at him in the changed light of what must have been quite late in the morning.

I'd slept. I'd delved into that depth of refreshing nothingness so deep that time stops, only to take you up again on the other side. One moment I'd lain listening to Jag's steadying breathing as the light outside was coming on, the next, time collected me rested and safe. Outside, the sea, which I could just hear, and the sun, which I could not.

Sliding out of bed, trying not to wake Jag, I slipped on my little bed-wear outfit before gently opening the door to the balcony. A Cornish wind whipped my hair as it white-rimmed the Atlantic that lapped at this most wild and lovely edge of England. The air wanted to be breathed. Cornwall blew the vestiges of sleep from me. The sun touched my face, still warm in the early autumn. My face felt touched, warmed, loved. This place, this fabulous and unlikely hotel, the untamed, miraculous coast, would always be like this, like my love, for me.

A phone beeped briefly from inside behind me. I turned. My mobile was on the table, but far enough away from Jag not to have broken his sleep. The double beep it had made let me know a text message had just been received. It immediately made me think of Beccs. I loved her. I wanted to tell her about myself, what was happening to me, how it could only change things for the better.

One more glance across the jagged line of the cliffs, and I went back inside to collect my phone and tiptoe into the bathroom to read the response to my message from last night. Beccs was still with me. I still had my best friend. Whatever had happened, whatever happened next between Jag and me, nothing could alter my relationship with Beccs. We'd survived Kirsty McCloud; nothing else could possibly be that detrimental to our friendship.

Taking one last glimpse at Jag as he slept on, I silently closed the bathroom door before turning on the light. An extractor fan whirred. I blinked in the false, fluorescent light.

The mobile, I now saw, was not mine – it was Jag's. I reached for the pull cord of the light switch, but didn't pull it. Although I knew I shouldn't, I couldn't resist pressing the Read button on Jag's phone to receive his message:

'HOW WAS ROOM SERVICE?'

I smiled, reading it again.

'HOW WAS ROOM SERVICE?'

I read it again and again. Something stirred in my anxiety banks as I looked again at the number of the sender. I didn't know the number, but felt I should – that I should be finding out who knew room service was available to Jag, who wanted to know how it was.

I called the number. It rang. It went into message mode, standard response from the line company. I shut it down, redialling immediately. It rang. It clicked. A voice, a man's voice, immediately said: 'Up late? Good man. Cornwall nice? How's she? Still out? Eh? Good man?'

The line went dead. I'd killed it, switching it down entirely, killing his voice, the voice I hated, the gut-stuttering machine-gun clatter of Ray Ray's stilted vocabulary coming at me, coming to get me, here, there, wherever I went.

My hair was all over the place from the wind outside. My face was white in the mirror, the eyes in my head blinking at what I'd just heard in sheer, desperate disbelief.

***

My face was white, Jag's brown as he slept. He'd be up late. 'Up late?' Ray had said, straight off, speaking to Jag's mobile, a number he recognised straight off, obviously. 'Cornwall nice?' Oh yes, Cornwall was nice all right.

I didn't know what to think. I think what I feel most of the time, that's my problem. Now I didn't know what to think because I was feeling everything all at once. There was something that made me want to feel sick – a feeling among all the others, all the scattered emotions of affection, desire, worry, anxiety and fear. Things were falling apart – that's how it felt. I was in the centre, holding on. Jag slept soundlessly, removed to one side, feeling nothing but his total relaxation, his satisfaction at what he had achieved.

I had to find out more. As quietly as I could, with my breath demanding more depth than I could silently give it, I gathered my few things, throwing on my top from yesterday, from last night, collecting my bag, putting Jag's mobile in there with my own. Taking what I hoped wouldn't be a last look at Jag sleeping, his upper half uncovered, I gently closed the door behind me.

A porter glanced at my trousers. They were red silk pyjama

bottoms taken from one of the rooms. He glanced at them before looking up at me. When he saw it was me, his look of recognition allowed me past. They let me wear anything I wanted. The clothes companies, the designers did it, so did the hotels. The restaurants would have let me wear their tablecloths if I'd wanted to. The butcher and baker would have draped me in red meat and bread. Solar Records would shroud me in tears.

I had to fight my emotions, trying to keep everything in place as I made my way to the hotel reception. A little boy and his mother stopped as I went by. 'That's that girl,' the boy said.

'Amy Peppercorn,' the mother replied. 'Yes, that's her. I wonder what she's doing here?'

The receptionist saw me coming, painting on a face for me. 'Good afternoon, Miss Peppercorn,' she smiled, her painted portrait too sweetly posed, head held just at a tilt as if she were curious at her own pleasure in seeing me.

'Good afternoon,' I said, glancing at the big wooden clock on the reception wall. I remembered my watch on the bedside cabinet upstairs. 'I'd like to pay – to settle the bill for the room, please?'

She took a moment to look at me. People did that, quite often, as if to confirm that I really did look like the Little Amy they'd seen and heard on their television sets. She smiled, taking a moment more, before shaking her head. 'That won't be necessary,' she said. 'It was paid for in advance. Rule of the hotel, at any time of the year.'

My thoughts flitted back to my wristwatch, ticking against the regular flow of Jag's slow breath. 'Oh,' I said. 'Can I ask who paid it?'

'Yes. I do believe – yes, it was your recording people. Here it is. Solar Records.'

'Of course,' I said, swallowing, trying to steady my voice.

'I expect,' I said, 'it was – when did they book the room, exactly?'

She looked on her records. She looked up, smiling brightly. She told me a date.

I smiled. 'Thank you,' I said, turning.

***

In the restaurant, sitting huge over little coffee cups, Minder Steve and my driver smoking cigarettes. I walked in on legs that just seemed to carry me where I knew they'd be, minder and driver, minding their own business.

Steve took an enquiring glance at the entrance, wondering for an instant, when I told him we were going, why Jag wasn't coming with us. As I didn't offer any explanation, he never took his enquiry any further than a single glance. 'Time to go,' I said, in a voice that sounded, to me, like somebody else's. 'I have to go home now.'

In two or three minutes we were in the car and pulling away from the redbrick building in which Jag still slept. I watched the hotel disappear as we went down the hill, the cliffs and sea shut off from view as simply as that – as one turn of the steering wheel, one depression of a right foot on to the car's accelerator pedal.

'I have to go home now,' I said to myself, in the back of the car. 'Take me home.'

Unwashed, unbreakfasted, unmedicated, I sat in the back in a daze, still wondering what had actually happened, with the date that the hotel room had been booked and paid for still reverberating through my brain. Solar Records, somebody from Solar, had booked the room some weeks before. In fact, the booking date corresponded exactly with the beginning of the first Little Amy Peppercorn UK tour.

I closed my eyes. We'd been booked in, from the very start, me and Jag, by someone at Solar. I hadn't known where we were going, but Jag did. So did someone at Solar.

Taking Jag's mobile from my bag, I turned it on and had another look at his messages:

'HOW WAS ROOM SERVICE?'

Before that:

'HOTEL ROOM ALL BOOKED 4U.'

That from the same source, the same mobile as the last message.

Jag had nineteen missed calls, with almost as many voice messages waiting. As I was looking them up, a call was coming in. It too came from that same source, that same mobile number I'd called only to hear the dread clatter of Raymond Raymond.

I opened the window and dropped the ringing mobile out, watching it bounce on the surface of the road before being flattened beneath the doubled-up tyres of the truck labouring forward some thirty or forty metres behind the Solar limousine.

Twenty-two

'You're late,' my dad told me, as if I didn't know.

I'd been sitting in the back of the car for hours wondering what had happened. But not really, because I knew. Ray had happened. It made me feel sick to think about it. So I tried to wonder what had happened, trying to trick myself into thinking I didn't know.

I knew. Even if I hadn't, I'd have seen it written on Leo's face when we stopped off at the McGregor and Fine mansion to get me a change of clothes. I couldn't go home in my silk pyjama bottoms and the little top I'd put on after last night's show. And I had to go home – I *had* to. There was nowhere else. All the way down the motorway, stopping only to visit the loo in the services to clean my teeth, remembering to take my medication with water, just to prove to myself how much I didn't need Jag, I'd been trying to make myself feel as if I was going home. Simply going home. The tour was over. It was finished. It had been a success. Time to go. Home.

But I was running home, with my tail well and truly between my legs. My head was being shaken almost from my shoulders as I tried not to think about what I couldn't avoid.

In the M and F house, running in, grabbing a handful of designer-wear to wear while trying not to be seen, everything I couldn't avoid was written all over Leo's face.

'What are you doing –' he said, then stopped. His surprised face told me. I already knew.

'What did you think you were doing?' he altered his position and said. 'Where did you go, you naughty girl?' he squirmed, back into his old act, his showbiz, kiss-on-each-cheek persona.

'Leo,' I said, 'don't treat me like that. You know where I went, Leo. Don't lie to me.'

He didn't say anything. Everything he didn't say confirmed everything I'd been trying not to think all the way down the motorway from the West country.

'Don't lie to me, Leo,' I tried to say without crying. 'Don't lie to me,' with a tear running from the corner of my eye. 'Herbal sleeping pills, Leo? Another lie. Don't do it to me any more. I thought you liked me more than that.'

He drew a deep, deep breath. 'Lovely,' he said, 'what can I say? I tried. Believe me, I tried. I told you not to love so much, didn't I? Didn't I try to tell you?'

'Leo,' I cried, trying not to, angry with my tear, angrily swiping it away, 'why does he have to do it? Why does he have to control everything and everybody? Why do they let him? Why do *you* let him, Leo? Why are you in it with him?'

'Sweet,' he said, about to shed a tear or two himself, 'don't you know? I can give you advice but I can't take it. Look at me. What can I do? I love him. I just can't stop –'

'Leo,' he said, stepping into view.

Leo died away. He shrank back into the shadows as his master appeared in a blaze of ever-black Solar anti-light. Raymond Raymond stepped forward, in control of the whole world. We all existed in his sight. He blinked, we disappeared. A dread omnipotent, he crushed Leo at a glance, giving me the pause in which to reinforce my hatred of him. Generous to a fault, at least he gave me that. Ray Ray was everything to a fault, as everything was at fault to Ray.

He didn't say anything. He had me, his face said for him.

This place – no M and F house at all. The lawns outside were Ray's home turf. It all belonged to him. Leo was his, to do with as he pleased. Jagdish belonged here. They were his eyes and ears, and a whole lot more. He had access to me, increasing my energy levels at will, sedating me, playing with my emotions like the musical instrument I was sure he'd have loved to have mastered, were he not so entirely musically bereft.

We looked long and hard at each other. He wanted to make me cry again, I knew it. He wanted my emotional submission. He used us all in this way. Lovely Leo was shivering in the shadows, unable to control himself. Ray was the all-powerful, magnificently angry man at the hub of the wheel of emotions he kept in place like the solar heart of the sun controlling the positions of its planets.

Ray wanted me to cry, but I hated him. Hating him, he made me hate myself, as his face told me, with the flicker of a semi-smile, that my hatred would do. Any extreme of emotion would suffice. Ray could always put it to good use.

He made me hate him. What else could I do? He was just too powerful. 'You're the star,' he said, eventually.

I couldn't speak. I rushed past him, clutching at my change of clothes. He let me pass, as if it didn't matter. As if I had nowhere else to go.

Twenty-three

'You're late,' my dad told me, as I came charging into the house. He said it as if I might not have realised I was late, that this was late afternoon and I'd been expected in the morning. But he said it without any question mark, as if his questions had already been taken care of.

I hadn't seen him for weeks. He turned and looked at me with no hint of worry. His voice settled easily over the strange furniture that had no relationship with my past. The whole house looked different, silently connected to now, or to some other time that couldn't include me. Nothing was the same. My dad was wearing clean clothes, all new. He looked clean and quite well groomed. His complexion was that of a younger man, or at least a man who ate and slept well. He smiled, properly satisfied, after weeks and weeks of his eldest daughter's absence.

'How you doing, Ames?' He smiled. Now he held out his arms, coming to hug me. There was an almighty smell of aftershave or deodorant that I recognised, but not from him. Not from him.

I pulled away, blinking at the changes all round me. The metamorphosis was complete, right down to the skirtings and the window frames. Our earlier lives had been eradicated. He smelled of someone else, someone I knew too well. My dad smelled the same as, but more strongly than, Jag.

As I stepped away from him, the door opened and my twin

sisters walked in on legs much sturdier than I remembered. They were both wearing shorts and little tiny tops with Little Amy Peppercorn written on them and a picture of me, singing. They stopped upon seeing me there, open-mouthed, staring up at me in awe.

'They can't believe it's you,' my dad said, stretching his back. 'They've watched you so often,' he said, grimacing, 'on TV, on video, they can't believe they've got a star for a sister. Isn't that right, girls? Is Amy Peppercorn your sister?'

'A-me,' one of them said. The other one's mouth let fall a neat line of dribble, which I was glad to see. It seemed to be the only thing I recognised.

'Look at your clothes,' I said to the girls. They looked down, surprised to see another image of me performing on their chests and over their bellies.

'A-me,' one said. The other one pointed at me.

'Why don't you give your sister a kiss?' my dad said to them.

There was a pause, after which one twin turned to the other and kissed her on the cheek.

'No,' my dad laughed. 'Give Amy a kiss. You haven't seen her for ages. Give your sister Amy a kiss, girls, why don't you?'

But the girls seemed to have got a picture of Amy Peppercorn plastered to the front of them that wouldn't allow any idea of me beyond the stage singing and the video image they sought to emulate. Beyond the image, confronted by the real thing, Jo and George Peppercorn were sisters to one another exclusively, two new Little Amy fans wearing everything but my mask of make-up.

'They've changed so much,' I said to my dad. 'I can hardly believe it.'

'Yes,' he said, proudly. He'd done this, his pride and bearing said, straightening his sore back in one. He hadn't done any of this for me, so was happy to care where he could, to the greatest effect.

'And the house,' he said. 'What do you think?' with his arms indicating a flourish left and right, taking in everything. For everything had changed. There was no pot or kettle or the slightest utensil surviving from my own childhood. Little Amy was here only in this most present guise, evident on my strange sisters' T-shirts, emotionally engineered to fit on any type or size of body.

'Good, eh?' my dad said. 'Come and see the new kitchen. Look. Big, isn't it?'

'Yes,' I said, looking right down into what would once have been half the length of our garden. 'It's big.'

'Your mum loves it,' he said. 'Doesn't she, girls?'

'*Does* Mum like it?' I said.

'She loves it,' my dad said. 'Anyway, you're late,' again telling, rather than asking me anything. 'Rebecca's been on the phone. She said your battery must be dead on your mobile, or something. Anyway, can you call her? You look well, anyway,' he said.

Yes, anyway, I looked well. I'd slept last night, thinking all the wrong things, resting in ignorance, believing in things that didn't exist – not really.

'You must have got a good night's sleep last night,' Dad said. 'Did you?'

'Yes,' I said.

Text to Beccs:

'CLL U 2MORO. 2DAY'S A DEAD DAY. LOVE. AMY.'

I couldn't call my best friend. The things I had to tell her were all about my emotions. And this was a dead day. My emotions were so scrambled I felt dizzy.

'You must be tired, though,' my dad said, 'after your journey?'

'Yes,' I said, confusing tiredness with mental fatigue. Just about everything Jag had ever said to me, all that Lovely Leo had to say kept flying into my face. Ray Ray's image simply looked at me, his knowing smile flickering malevolently. Ray knew everything. His knowing was hateful, spiteful. He used every scrap of knowledge cynically, exploiting it to his every advantage, using emotions as if he were modelling them to fit his plan. Jag had fitted in where and when, according to Ray's plan. Leo was planned entirely. There then, little Amy P., contained, subtly caged but incarcerated, unable to see, but looked upon, examined, put to best use.

Oh God, I was a fool! Such a fool! What an idiot! Not to see the bars of that cage when there they were in front of me, too glaringly obvious for anyone with half a mind to see.

'You must be tired, though,' my dad said, 'after your journey?'

I had to agree. I had to be, to be as I was, left like this with no one to talk to, not even Beccs, now I felt like such a fool. I felt trapped. The house surrounding me did just the same – it too encapsulated. No home should feel like this. No home seemed to exist here, no place to which I could have run and hidden, to have cried into the shoulder of my old self and mourned the passing of my childhood into a better, more exciting and fuller life. Instead I suffered the reverse, duped into giving it all away too cheaply, for commercial success, for money. That's what it all boiled down to. Money transfigured the house I'd always lived in, spraying my dad in the juice that Jag stank of, the sickly sweet scent of ambition. Look at my sisters, the way they were being weaned to it, swept along as innocently and as unquestioningly as my dad. How stupid we all looked from the other side.

I had to text Beccs instead of calling her, to take my emotions and make something other than stupidity out of them. Oh Beccs – I'd let her down. It wasn't out there, the life we'd expected with our easy laughter. Our friendship still depended upon some sort of success. Beccs was still at school; the onus was all on me.

***

How far I had to go to reach my bedroom, the one room that might still contain the remains of my beginnings, when the front door was being knocked almost through and the bell rung, ringing with a chime that appalled me by playing the tune of *If Ever*. My dad came bustling as I froze on the stairs. 'That'll be the door,' he said, impressed by the urgency of the knocking and chiming.

I stood still on the stairs, transfixed by that same urgency and the horribly cheapened rendition of my biggest hit so far. A certain mocking attitude in the tune, a definite ambitiousness in the rapping of the doorknocker warned me, turned me, tense with knowing expectation to see who my dad would so readily admit to our house.

Again, my father's prior, insider knowledge let him lack surprise, opening the door, stepping back automatically to allow Jag in.

Jag was wearing jeans and a shirt, dressed as I'd never seen him, looking as different as if everything had changed.

'Someone to see you!' my dad turned and shouted, calling up to my room. 'Oh,' he said, surprised to discover me still on the stairs. 'You're there,' he said.

'Yes,' I said, stepping down, 'I'm here.'

'Hello, Amy,' Jag said.

'Hello,' I said.

My dad closed the front door. 'I'll, ah, leave you to it,' he said, melting away guiltily.

We stood in the hall, Jag and me. He noticed me looking at his clothes. 'You look different,' I said.

'Well, I'm not,' he said. 'I'm not, Amy. I'm just the same.'

'Well, I'm not,' I said, 'am I?'

He was blinking quickly as I looked into his face. He couldn't look at me. 'I had to come back on the train,' he said. 'Do you still have my mobile?'

'No,' I said.

He didn't ask after his phone any more. I didn't have it, neither did he. 'I had to see you,' he said, reaching out to touch me.

I flinched, moving away from his hand with distaste.

'Amy,' he said, softly.

'No,' I said. 'Don't.'

'It doesn't have to be like this. Nothing's changed.'

'Oh? Nothing's changed? Is that so?'

'I know,' he said. 'I know. There's Ray. But there's always Ray. There always was.'

'Not as far as I was concerned.'

'No, maybe not. But he was always there.'

'Oh, sure. Vitamins and minerals from you, herbal sleeping tablets from Leo? What *was* in those things? Nothing legal, that I do know.'

'It doesn't make any difference,' Jag said.

'Oh, really?'

'No, Amy, listen. What we said – everything I said to you I meant. Ray can't change that.'

I shook my head as his hand came towards me again.

'Amy,' he said, 'I meant everything I said. Did you?'

'I wanted you to keep me safe, Jag. I wanted that.'

'And I did, didn't I?'

'So you think keeping me safe means wearing something, is that it? Is that all? You were supposed to be what I had that wasn't part of – wasn't what he – what everything Ray does to – to –'

'Amy,' he said, coming towards me. He tried to kiss me, where Ben had once kissed me and I'd missed it. Well, now Jag's kiss missed too, as it would never reach me again.

'No!' I said. 'You won't get near me, Jag,' I said, deliberately. 'Do you know why? Shall I tell you why?'

He nodded, serious-faced.

'I'll tell you why. Because if you get near me, *he's* near me. I'll never be able to put it out of my mind. Do you see? You should have kept me safe. I can't – you're not it, Jag. You're a big mistake. Now, get out,' I said, incredibly calmly. 'Go away. We'll see each other again, but it'll never be the same. Do you understand? Never the same again.'

He nodded.

'Get out, now,' I said, holding the door open for him. I shook my head as he went to say something. He looked down. 'Goodbye, Jag.'

He went, without another word. I didn't watch him go, hardly able to bring myself to look at him now. The door closed, also incredibly calmly, behind him.

I looked at my hand, expecting it to be shaking. It was dead still. I felt for my heart. It wasn't there. A black hole only.

My dad's head appeared at the other door, a question on his face. I looked too calmly at him for him to face me. He backed away.

The hall where Ben had kissed me that evening, years ago it felt, had changed. There was an unworn carpet on the stairs.

We had a new banister. There was a little window halfway up with stained glass in it – that hadn't been there before. My sisters were walking and talking, looking at me like some kind of unapproachable idol. Where was I? I felt lost here, casting round in a house I couldn't recognise for something, anything left of me untainted by the pestilent Solar wind.

***

I ran upstairs, throwing open my bedroom door. The door was new, but my old room could still be there as always, behind it. I threw open the new door, praying that I wouldn't discover another new, entirely unwelcoming place. But there it was, untouched, like the only remnant I could find of the real Amy Peppercorn. There was my old bed, my old furniture, carpet, curtains. All untouched as yet. An unaffected haven waiting for me to make it back before my own dad and Raymond Raymond could complete my deconstruction.

The only ugly interloper, that which flapped through the half-open door of my wardrobe: designer-labelled, skimpy-stringed, my wardrobe showed no entrance into another, enchanted ice-world, but clamoured to be let into this one. The designer-wear jostled to be allowed through, to be given rein over this last tiny remnant of my self-preservation. They were suddenly horrible, these things, with what they wanted to bring in. That, *like* that, was exactly how they wanted me to be, and nothing else, clambering empty-armed through my wardrobe door like dead nightmare arms of vacant vitality and a horrible, too potent strength.

I threw them out. Great bundled armfuls of garments fell in a heap on to the landing floor. I grabbed them, dragging them out as if they were kicking and screaming. I showed no mercy. I was wild. There was an anger biting at my jaw. The wardrobe doors thumped, I thumped them back. Thump! Thump! Thump!

My dad must have heard. He must have, but chose to do nothing about it. Good. Because he was part of it. I'd have thrown the whole pile over his head. In fact, I wanted to. I wanted to throw it all at all of them, chucking it back in their faces. Because this was what they'd done to me. This was what they'd done – as I threw another armful on to the growing pile on the landing outside the loo. This! It was their fault, all of this. And this! And this!

I threw it all out. I wanted to scream, really I did. Didn't want to cry, but didn't scream. Cried. Tears running down my face as I threw out the last of the clothes, leaving just the one hanger swinging. On it, my old school uniform.

I'd done my GCSEs in this. Still it hung there, skirt, jacket, shirt, tie, complete. Like a relic of what I was when I thought I could become – I don't know what. Anything maybe. Anything but unhappy.

The clothes, the Solar garments I stood in joined the pile outside the toilet. I stood in front of the mirror, watching the schoolgirl with the old, caked mascara, the blackened tears, full lips with darkened tear-tracks traced into the corners.

On my dressing table, my cleansing creams, my cotton pads. On my face, plenty to be cleansed, to be scrubbed away. I scrubbed at it, pulling at my eyelids, dragging off the over-caked remnants of a poor disguise, revealing a spoiled simplicity hidden below.

With all the old make-up removed, there wept Amy, as if she was back. I looked at her in the mirror. I wanted to scream; she couldn't. She couldn't do it. She wept, looking back at me for what I'd let them do to her.

My dad knocked at my door. He waited. The girl in the

mirror didn't flinch. Another knock, but too softly for his hand. That wasn't him.

The mirror girl disappeared as I moved away. I crossed my room in a few steps, throwing open the door.

She looked at me. 'Oh Amy!' my mum said.

The mirror girl looked up at her and cried.

'Oh Amy!' my own mother said, crying too, to see what might have been reflected there. 'What have you done?'

I dashed into her arms.

Twenty-four

'I thought you'd gone away from me,' she said, as we sat together on my bed.

'Mum, no! You were just never – you weren't there.'

'I wanted to be,' she said. 'I didn't think you needed me any more.'

'Oh Mum,' I said, as we held on to each other. Beccs was the best of my friends, but my mum was my best friend.

'You're not going to find what you're looking for in the wardrobe,' she told me.

My school uniform fitted me as it always had, but I couldn't get the feel for it. It belonged back on the hanger, wrapped for posterity in crinkly cellophane. My mum knew.

'It isn't what's supporting you,' she said.

And I could see; she was my mother.

'You can come back to me,' she said.

I cried. I could come back to her. I could come home. My mum said.

'I can come home, too,' she said.

She cried too. We both did.

* * *

'Was it – all right?' she asked. She wept. 'It was safe, wasn't it?'
I nodded. We wept.

***

'I thought Little Amy Peppercorn didn't need me,' she said.

***

'But I love you,' I said.

***

'I thought,' she said, 'that even the twins didn't need me any more. You've seen them.'
'They're like Dad,' I said. 'They're all still babies.'
'I'd lost sight of where I belonged,' she said.
'Me too,' I said.

***

'We belong here,' we said. We both said it, my mum and me.

***

My dad came up at one point, with some tea. 'You two are having a long chat,' he said.
'Yes,' my mum said. 'Yes, we are.'

***

'They used me,' I said, crying again. 'They used me and used me.'

'Use them back,' my mum said. 'Do what they do. Do it better.'

I almost felt that we should be getting out my maths books. Do it better, she said, my mum, my teacher. She was strong for me, as she'd always been. For a while I'd let her go, without realising it. Now I realised it, recognising the consequences. Next time – next time I'd do it better. You watch.

⁂ Twenty-five

'Raymond's been on the blower,' my dad said. 'He wants to know –'

'Tell him I'll be there,' I interrupted. 'Get on the *blower*, Dad, and tell Ray I'll be doing the concert. Tell him it's still for Geoff Fryer and for charity, despite what he's done to it. Tell him that, would you?'

My dad blinked at me, wiping his mouth with the back of his hand.

⁂

'Leo,' I said, as he answered his mobile.

'Lovely!' he cried. 'Oh, my Sweet. Where are you?'

'I'm at home.'

'Well, shouldn't you be –'

'Leo, shut up and listen.'

'Oh, how lovely.'

'Just listen, Leo. I want you to do something for me. And you're going to do it, do you hear me?'

'I hear you. I might not do it, but I hear you.'

'Leo, I just want you to contact somebody for me. Somebody I want to talk to, urgently.'

'Who?'

'Wait, and I'll tell you. I'll tell you and you'll tell Ray. I know you will.'

'Well, I might –'

'Leo, don't. I don't care what you tell Ray. Tell him everything. I know you have to. Just do as I say. Ray won't stop me. Believe me. He won't stop me, no matter what you say to him.'

'I won't say anything if I don't want to.'

I almost laughed. 'Good,' I said. 'And I have to see you soon. We've got a lot of work to do before the concert.'

'The concert? You're doing it?'

'Oh yes, I'm doing it all right. Don't worry about that.'

'Are you all right?' my mum asked.

'Yes, Mum,' I said. 'I am.'

'Are you all right?' I asked. I was lying awake on my bed, picturing him lying on his.

He didn't sound at all surprised to hear me. In fact, he didn't sound as if anything at all *could* surprise him, particularly.

I had lain awake for hours thinking of this moment. Not just this moment – all the moments leading up to right now. But remembering wouldn't lead me conveniently on into the present, but tumbled in a chaos of deceit and lies. Or if not lies, then abused truths, which are often worse. My mum had asked me if I was all right. As far as she was concerned, as far as my relationship with my mum was concerned, I was all right. If I had that, I could cope with this. And if I didn't sleep, if I lay awake longing for one of Leo's non-organic sleeping pills until the early morning, then that was how it had to be. At least this was mine, this blank dawn, opening like a tired eye upon the world.

Yes, I still loved the world. I'd told Beccs time and again how much I loved. I'd been filled with love and the expectation of love. Now the expectation had all but vanished, love stayed with me. Jag had done me dreadful harm. I was hurting. Oh yes, I hurt.

I hurt so much I could have come all to pieces. My best friend Beccs was waiting for news of me. I was going to dash our understanding into as many pieces as my poor fragmented emotions. Beccs had been there with me, all the way. I felt as if I'd let her down. I should have done better by her.

My mum had told me it wasn't so. 'She's your friend,' she said. I loved my mum. Without her – without her, I couldn't have – all the things I had to face I couldn't have, without her. I had so much to do. If she hadn't been there, if I'd had to rely on my dad – well!

'Mum?' I'd said.

She had cried for me, with me; then we'd stopped.

'Mum? Please – please make Dad take that stupid, stupid door chime down.'

The thing had played a plinky-plonky version of *If Ever* maybe as many as twelve or thirteen times during the course of the evening as people kept turning up at our door. 'That'll be the door!' my dad would shout up the stairs, every time.

'Doesn't it drive you mad?' I asked my mum.

She laughed. 'Of course it does. But it's just your dad, isn't it? I'll get him to choose another tune.'

'Get him to choose another doorbell,' I said.

I couldn't have made my dad understand. My mum could. She did. She did everything. She's my mum. I love her.

She did everything – everything but make me sleep. She told me I should. 'See to it all in the morning,' she said.

I didn't tell her about the pills I'd been taking from Leo and Jag. The pills were light and dark, energy and rest. But those things should have always been with me naturally. I was as organic as the natural world. Surely I should sleep and laugh and love unassisted, without tears and regret?

All night I think I cried. Jag would have tried to kiss me in the hall last night, but it would have missed me by a mile. I hadn't yet spoken to Beccs. My mum said I hadn't let my best friend down. My mum was my best friend. I had. *I had.*

Come very early morning, my mobile beeped, downloading all the text messages I'd been sending Ben:

'CALL ME.'

'CALL ME!'

'CALL ME!!'

'CALL ME!!!'

They must have trailed down the air-line in a series request, gathering speed and urgency as they took their turn. I quickly called him before he could turn off again.

'Ben! Ben, are you there?'

'I'm here,' Ben's voice suddenly said.

I paused. It was Ben, his voice, exactly as I remembered it after all we'd been through. 'Are you all right?' I asked. We'd been through so much. The mobile phone lines connected our voices across everything that had so separated us.

'Are you?' he said.

'Yes,' I said. 'I am now.'

'I suppose you want me to thank you –' he started to say.

'Ben! Don't! I don't want you to do anything.'

'No,' he said. 'I didn't want you to, either. They ought to put me away. I don't know what I'm doing here. It isn't real.'

'Yes it is, Ben. You're home, aren't you? That's real, believe me. That's as real as it gets.'

'Yeah? For you, maybe.'

'And for you, Ben.'

'No. This is a dream. I don't believe in it.'

'Ben, don't. Geoff wouldn't want this.'

'No? You know, do you?'

'So do you. Come on. You knew Geoff better than I did. He wouldn't want you to suffer.'

'Well, he can't stop me, can he?' he said.

We said nothing for a while. A statement like that, it ticks on and on in the air, in your ear, through your head.

'He wouldn't want you to suffer, Ben,' I said, 'Neither would his mum. Go and see her. Talk to her. We're all doing the show for Geoff –'

'No! Forget it. Call your lawyers. Tell them not to bother. It isn't worth the bother.'

'Wait, Ben. Listen. That song you sent me, *Last Chance Remark*. Where is it? Wait a minute.' I scrambled, remembering when I'd placed it, for safekeeping, under my mattress. 'Here, Ben. This:

There's no place to turn here
No going back, it
Has no reverse gear.
So forward madly
Till you stack it
Take what's coming
Fortune's packet,
Death-defying,
But you can't hack it.

'That's – it's wrong, Ben. It isn't finished.'

'Yes it is,' he said.

'No, Ben, it isn't. It's only just started. Come to the gig – the show for Geoff. They're closing off one of the parks in London –'

'I know.'

'Will you, then? Please, Ben?'

'Amy – I can't. I – Geoff didn't – you didn't see him. I did. You didn't. You can remember him. I can't forget him.'

'I can't forget him. Every – all the –'

'I can't forget – what I did to him. What I did to Geoff!'

Ben. I could have cried for him. I would have kissed him if I could have touched him over the phone lines, but I think he'd have missed it.

We laughed!

Beccs and me, me and Beccs. We laughed and laughed. It was so – I could have cried. But we laughed! Beccs. She's – I can't tell you what she means to me.

She tried on some of my clothes. She looked good. She was still playing football, but looked leaner, more muscular. 'Are you sure?' she said.

'Your legs are fantastic,' I said.

'No one's seen Ben,' she told me, looking at herself in my bedroom mirror. 'His mum's really worried about him.'

'I know,' I said.

Beccs looked at me in the mirror.

'Will you wear that?' I said. 'It looks perfect. You wear that, I'll wear this.'

Beccs looked back into the mirror at herself, then at me. 'Could have been worse,' she smiled slyly. 'He could have been ugly.'

What a laugh! We were in the papers, Jag and me – pictures of us dancing, in each other's arms. A close-up of us kissing.

'I wish he *was* ugly,' I said.

'So do I,' Beccs said, looking at me in the mirror out of the corner of her eye. 'Lucky cow!'

What a laugh! Beccs brought it all back into perspective for me. I could feel my relief – I could feel my mum's relief as she listened to us laughing from outside my bedroom door. I could hear the altered tune of our door chime. I could feel my mother's rekindled interest in the house, our home, with the furniture she was suggesting changing, with my dad's relieved mock-disapproval. The twins were having a rare old punch-up. Something smashed – it sounded expensive. The girls were screaming for their mum. They were my sisters.

Beccs was a better friend than I deserved. Nobody deserves friendship like this. This was just luck. I don't believe in fate or anything like that – all you can do is concentrate on your good luck and work to deny your bad. Beccs was to my good side, most definitely. She deserved my concentration. All the bad I was working to deny.

'Oh, that's good,' I said. 'That looks really good.'

'Skimpy or what?' Beccs said, looking at herself in my wardrobe mirror. She was wearing a little leather skirt with a yellow top with yellow wrist and biceps bands connected at the back of her arms with a strip of the same fabric, like an intermittent sleeve. She looked great. She was a footballer, but all the weight she'd lost hadn't come back. Not all of it, anyway. She was a lot heavier, or so she said; but it looked like toned muscle, very sleek and powerful.

'You look great,' I said.

'I don't think I can dare,' she said. 'Not like this.'

'Of course you can,' I said. 'Anyway, who's going to see you?'

She looked at me.

We laughed.

* * *

'Leo?' I said, into my mobile. 'Did you get through to her? And she's expecting my call? Good. Now, listen, this is what we're going to do.'

'Hello, Amy.'

'Hello, Mrs Fryer. Thanks for seeing me.'

'It's a pleasure to see you again, Amy. I see you just about everywhere, anyway. You have been busy, haven't you?'

'Yes,' I said. 'Yes, I have.'

Twenty-six

Were you there? I hope you were. If you were part of that crowd in the park that day, if you were in the audience, you'd have seen it all. You'd have seen the stage set, the huge speakers, the wide screens. Even if you weren't there, you might have seen it live on TV, or on the news, or repeated later that evening on Channel Five. The chances are you did see it – or some of it, at least. You probably saw me in my white, my all-white costume, with a white leather skirt and a white banded top like the one in yellow Beccs had tried on in my bedroom. You probably saw the signs:

Solar Records Presents
LITTLE AMY PEPPERCORN
On Behalf of Cancer Research
In Association With
The Geoffrey Fryer Trust

If you did see it, you saw Solar Records presenting a Little Amy P. with Raymond Raymond's signature unseen but written large at the bottom like a broadcasted copy of my five-year Solar contract. What you didn't see was little Amy and a silent Jag and a V-line of nervous dancers waiting under the stage for the introductory explosion to propel us upwards into the smoky light. Even had you seen us, you probably wouldn't have sensed my resentment of Ray Ray's signature-force superimposed upon the modesty of what this event should have been. This was supposed to have been words of farewell to a school friend, a friend, a loved son.

I was to burst on to the stage in an explosion of indignation, belting out *Proud* as if I really was. But now the line, *But they don't know you like I do/They don't show through like you do* contained any amount of newly introduced irony, with me glancing at Jag as if he really was showing through. Which he was. He danced in the bog-standard line like any other dancer, too shamed to follow me into the fore, too subdued to sing *Proud* with me with any pride.

I spat words like fire:

I'm proud of you.
I'm proud of you.

If you were in that audience, I hope you bit them up and spat them back:

I'm proud of you!

Yes, we did *Proud* proud, that audience and me, with the dancers doing what dancers do and nothing more. Everything else was up to me. I made and maintained contact with the audience, my fans:

I'm proud of you!

And I was. I have to admit it. Not that I mind admitting it. The pride I thought I'd have to feel in others, in people like Jag, was all mine. I was proud that these people, all these people were here to see me.

I sang. I danced. No props, no pills. As organic as the world I loved, I lifted my audience with me until all of us were sailing somewhere high enough off the ground not to feel our feet.

From *Proud* we went straight into *The Word on the Street*, pausing only for a few beats to allow the applause to let the sound back through. The set, huge as it was, was filled with my little body and big voice. Solar Records had scored Ray Ray's signature tunes carefully, using the age-old talents of McGregor and Fine coupled with the new-look image of little me and this voice of mine. So far Geoff Fryer was represented here only as the mention of a trust fund set up in his name for charity. Not good enough. Too much showbiz, not enough sincerity for my liking or for Geoff's memory.

So I stopped the song, shutting it down halfway through, signalling the musicians to fall silent. Stopping the dancers in their tracks. Glancing at Jag. Nothing more.

I turned, looked out across a sea of expectant faces. I took a deep breath. 'I feel like screaming,' I said into the hand-mike. 'I feel like screaming so often nowadays.' A ripple of applause passed through the crowd. The faces looked back at me. 'Listen,' I said. 'Let me tell you something. See that sign? Solar Records Presents – In Association with The Geoffrey Fryer Trust? Geoff Fryer was my friend. He died. His mum's here today. Mrs Fryer's here with us today. We only wish Geoff could be. If he was, I'm sure he'd want us to have a good time. Geoff *is* here, as part of what we're doing. I'll never forget him.'

I looked out across the silent sea of the audience. I smiled. 'So we're gonna have a good time. I've sung songs for Geoff in the past. Today, everything's for him. If you read about what happened to Geoff in the papers, don't believe everything you read.' I glanced at Jag. He looked away from me into the audience. 'Don't believe them!' I shouted. 'YOU WANNA HAVE A GOOD TIME?'

The crowd erupted.

'YOU WANNA HAVE A REALLY GOOD TIME?' I shouted.

'The crowd shouted back.

'YOU FEEL LIKE SCREAMING?'

They screamed.

'DON'T BELIEVE EVERYTHING YOU READ!' I yelled. 'BUT BELIEVE THIS – this concert for my friend, for Geoff – here, live on stage, please welcome a personal friend of mine. Please welcome, here now, COURTNEY SCHAEFFER!'

***

As Courtney came out on to the stage, the crowd went wild. She was wearing white, like me, but in a slightly different design. We blasted into a version of one of her early hits, *Survive*.

The press cameras were flashing almost continuously, drenching us in light as we marched in different directions across the stage, exchanging hand-claps as we passed in the centre. She looked fantastic. She was taller than me, naturally, but she wasn't tall – she just looked it.

I'd like to be able to say I didn't think of Kirsty McCloud at any time during the performance, but I can't. All through *Survive*, I was smiling at the picture Kirsty must be getting on her TV screen, if she wasn't in the crowd, of Courtney and me doing an uncoordinated version of the number she'd so energetically rehearsed and so badly executed. It made me smile to think of the steam that would be rising from her reddening face, dampening her long blonde hair.

The press were recording every move on still cameras, the TV stations filming and broadcasting live the arch enemies, Courtney and me hand in hand to take our applause together. We hugged. 'Well done,' she said, or rather mouthed, as we couldn't hear anything.

'Thank you,' I said, hugging her.

The cameras snapped us up.

I signalled to the band behind us. Lovely Leo lurked on the outskirts, fiddling with a synthesiser keyboard. Jag and the other dancers waited to be told what to do. Good. Jag would always have to wait to be told from here on, at least as far as I was concerned. My signal started *The Word on the Street* again, into which Courtney and I launched, taking turns alternately, line after line:

Courtney: *The word is out there*
Me: *The word is on the street*
Courtney: *There is no doubt there*
Me: *Is a life so incomplete*

Alternating like that, until:

Courtney and me: *And our love's back on the right track*
Courtney and me: *Now the word is on the street.*

We went through the lyric, alternately, together. Our voices were so very different, but, brought together, sounded harmonious, pitched perfectly one against the other. We ran round the lyric once more until the instrumental bit was supposed to sail us into the inevitable last repetition of the same lines. But that didn't happen. Instead:

'Please welcome,' I cried, 'on stage, my friend –'

'And my friend,' Courtney came in unexpectedly, 'BECCS BRADLEY!' she shrieked.

And Beccs skipped on wearing her yellow outfit to a rapturous applause that kind of knocked her back into a nervous shyness.

'BECCS BRADLEY!' I cried, running to her, taking her by the hand, thrusting a mike into it.

The word is out there,
The word is on the street,

Beccs rapped, looking in complete horror and fear across the ocean of humanity spread out before her. Nobody knew her, but the audience had welcomed her on stage as if she was one of the best-known girl rappers in the country. She held on, love her, running through the rap words she'd learned:

There is no doubt there
Is a life so incomplete

She began to relax as she went on, starting to move across the stage as she had when rapping with Car Crime a lifetime ago. Geoff's lifetime ago. But here we were, with Beccs, my friend, growing in confidence as she went on into the new lines we'd devised between us:

But now the word is on the street
Ben, you're coming back.
And life's got a wrong and right track
And all the people we could meet
Are never wholly good or bad
But deluded, tricked or made sad,
But the word is on the street
My friend
That death is never
Friendship's end
If you don't let it go –
But if you do
You'll never know
The word that's on the street
For you,
For you,
The word that's on the street.

With Courtney and me coming in with Beccs at this point:

The word that's on the street
For you,
For you,
The word that's on the street.

I was, I have to admit, thinking of Kirsty again as we three, Courtney, Beccs and me, took the applause at the end. We were holding hands, holding each other's hands in the air. Beccs was in the middle. I held her hand so tight, so tight. She held mine back. We smiled, grinned at each other. Beccs grinned with Courtney.

I stepped forward. 'This,' I said, looking out, feeling something, something huge and wonderful inside me like love. Yes, I still loved the world. Yes. 'This,' I said, 'is a song for Geoff, especially for him. It always has been, right from the start.'

But I didn't sing it. Not to start with. Courtney came forward, stood next to me. She started to sing:

You would seize the day for me,
Keep the night away for me.
Make the darkness light for me,
The noble sun ignite for me,
If ever, if ever you were here.

I watched her sing *If Ever*, the song for Geoff. *My* song for Geoff. Everybody's song, but sung by Courtney Schaeffer for my friend. Beccs stepped away. I stood next to Courtney. The audience watched us. Press cameras were flickering continuously.

But nothing is forever now I know
The sunrise and the day will go.
As the sun will burn to death one day
To be with you where you have gone
Where suns and stars have never shone.

With the camera flashes flickering like brief suns and stars in our eyes, we sang together, together:

Oh, you would seize the day for me

We sang together, but then with Courtney choosing to step away, to take her place with Beccs behind me, as I finished the song for Geoff alone. For Geoff:

Once more
Just one more day to keep

I looked over at the enclosure by the side of the stage where my mum and dad stood with Geoff's mum and dad, with Mr Fryer holding one of my sisters in each of his big burly arms. Nobody cried. I sang:

As darkness makes its way to sleep
To know that you've been near again
(Deep breath. Last line. For Geoff.)
I'd never, ever shed a tear again.

My powerful voice fell to a passionate silence, a beat or two, before I shouted: 'That's for you, Geoff!'

My sisters bounced and clapped all over Mr Fryer. Mrs Fryer did not cry. She did nothing. Sometimes, nothing is the most important, most poignant thing to do. All round, for as far as the eye could see the park, people clapped. Mrs Fryer maintained a wonderful, beautiful dignity. I bowed towards her, closing my eyes. Such bravery made me feel so – yes, so small. Feeling small isn't a question of personal size, it's a matter of emotional perspective. Whatever Solar Records had done to me through Jag, through every other control device, my discomfort was as nothing compared to the dignity of Geoffrey Fryer's mother. I bowed to her, with my eyes closed.

***

'COURTNEY SCHAEFFER!' I yelled, as Courtney left the stage. Feeling small was not something I was particularly suited to. *Being* small I was perfect at, but feeling it wasn't me – not for long, anyway.

'Courtney Schaeffer!' I yelled again. 'Isn't she great?'

The audience appreciated her, at least right now. Right now, they thought she was great. So did I.

'Listen!' I shouted to the crowd. 'LISTEN! I'm proud of you!'

They whistled and clapped. The applause grew.

'Ben! If you're out there, I'm proud of you! Can you hear me?'

The audience screamed back at me. Beccs laughed. She was wearing the same as me but in a different colour. I loved being on stage with her, singing with her again.

'Listen!' I screamed. 'We've got a new song for you! This is a song by Ben Lyons. Ben, if you're out there – I know you are – I'm Proud of You.

***

We stood side by side, Beccs and me. The lights all came on. The set was flooded in light, burning out even the Solar flickering of the press photographers. I sang slowly, the lights going down again around me, with the best of my friends standing next to me:

Love isn't always what it seems,
Last lines pen a maniac's dreams.
Lights out (with the lights going out)
life's lost in the dark,

When you're awake you're facing it,
You're all through with racing it,
All that's left is the last chance remark.

A pause, briefly, before I screamed: 'NO!'

Spotlights blazed, as if shocked by the all-of-a-sudden finality of my scream. 'No!'

Beccs came back into the light. She rapped:

Are you broken down boy,
You a loser?
Fortune's clown boy,
Beggar or chooser?
Wake up in a fit
You know what you are
Get up and run for it
You know you'll go far.

I sang:

Last lines to a lover's lost dreams
Lights out, life's lived in the dark.
Dread isn't always what it seems,
When you're racing it
You're awake and you're facing it,
Love lives in your last chance remark.

Beccs rapped:

There's no place to turn here
No going back, it
Has no reverse gear.
So forward madly
You won't stack it
Take what's coming
Fortune's packet

Death-defying
You can hack it!

I sang:

Lost lines pen a lover's last dreams,
Light on, life sees through the dark.
Death isn't always what it seems
When you're racing it,
You're alive and you're facing it
Love lives – it's your last chance remark!

'Love lives!' I screamed.

Beccs rapped: 'We're proud of you!'

Together: 'We're Proud of You!'

Us, with the audience: 'We're Proud of You!'

Us, the audience, Mr and Mrs Fryer, my mum and dad: 'We're Proud of You!'

No Jag.

'We're Proud of You!'

'We're Proud of You!'

No Jag.

'We're Proud of You!'

'We're Proud of You!'

I screamed.

'WE'RE PROUD OF YOU!'

Twenty-seven

I was back on the Frank Fisher chat show. Lovely Leo had been organising everything for me. Until today, Ray Ray had been nowhere to be found, no doubt deep in discussion with his lawyers as to just what would happen if I chose to break my contract with Solar. The only decision I'd made was not to make any decisions yet. Not just yet.

Frank Fisher was grinning at me. 'You and Courtney, on stage together – now that was a turn-up for the books, wasn't it?'

I smiled back into his face with enough of my own confidence to confront him as he tried to affront me. Everyone was on to me. I had to go into hiding in a safe house – Beccs's actually – staying in her spare room for a few days. The press were everywhere. Raymond had texted me just before Frank's show:

'YOU WIN! M AND F WANT TO WORK WITH YOU. IT WORKS. CALL ME. R.R.'

I win. When you lose, you can win. My mum had said to me, in my room, with me in my old school uniform and she in her old-school self: 'There are two types of person in this world, Amy. There are those that make things happen, and those that have things happen to them.'

'Things happen to everyone,' I'd said.

'Yes,' she had replied, 'but that doesn't need to be the end to it. The things that happen to you can be the start of the things that you'll make happen.'

'And what type are you?' I asked.

'You tell me.'

I looked into her strong, intelligent face, a mixture of tears and determination. 'I know which type you are,' I said, 'but what type is Dad?'

She had laughed. So did I. 'More importantly,' she had said, 'what type are you?'

***

I win.

'You and Courtney,' Frank grinned, happy, or so he said, to have me back on his show. 'You and Courtney on stage together, singing, high-fiving – well, you were high-fiving. She was sort of middle or low-fiving.' He paused for laughter. I was small, but Frank Fisher couldn't make me feel it. 'I thought you and she didn't like each other?'

'Did you?' I said.

'Well, yes. In the papers, the two of you looked like life-long enemies. You've changed all that, haven't you?'

'I've changed a lot of things,' I said.

He smiled. 'Yes. Very successful tour, I hear. Congratulations. And – I hear – or I saw in the papers, your name – or rather your body linked with that of a certain dancer in your company?'

'I've changed a lot of things,' I said again.

'Oh. So it's off, is it?'

I laughed. 'Let's just say that he's been offered a part in a West End show and he'd be mad not to accept.'

'Right,' he smiled at the juicy morsels of my private life. Frank was like an expansion of the papers I liked least – the type that make news out of gossip and try to embellish the news with as much gossip as they can possibly dig up. Frank

Fisher and these papers would make victims of us, of people like Courtney Schaeffer and me and Ben and Geoff, and Jag as well, if we let them.

'So what's next?' he said. 'The album's selling well, a successful tour behind you. Back to school, is it?'

'No,' I said, 'not yet. I'm working hard. There are lots of things I have to do.'

'Your old mate,' Frank said with a leer, steering the interest back to my private life, 'your ex, the carboy? Back inside, isn't he?'

I smiled back at Frank as he smiled at me. If you think a smile's a friendly symbol, you've never looked at the animosity in the irregular rows of Frank Fisher's teeth, nor smelt the antique nicotine directed your way in brown, serpentine malevolence.

'Well, Frank,' I said, 'there are two types of people in this world.'

'Those that split people up into two types,' he said, quick as a serpent, 'and those that don't.'

I laughed along with everybody else. Everybody else always laughed – that was what they were there for. And it was funnier, and much more comfortable, to be on Frank's side of the laughter.

'There are those people that make things happen,' I continued, 'and those that have things happen to them.'

We sat, Frank and I, eye to eye, our fixed opposing smiles saying much, much more than we did.

'And which type is Little Amy Peppercorn?' Frank said, finally.

I smiled as hard as I could – harder than Frank dared, harder, even, than Raymond Raymond, who grinned like a crocodile.

***

'What *are* you going to do now?' Beccs asked.

We were in the car on the way to a restaurant – just me and Beccs, after the Frank Fisher Show. We were wearing – we were wearing some nice clothes from Beccs's wardrobe, not mine, for the restaurant, for a nice night out together. It felt like such a relief to be out with her like this right now – easy together, able to talk about anything and everything now that her cousin wasn't bending her to fit.

'I'm going to get to Ben,' I said.

'Yes,' she said. 'So am I.'

Ben had been arrested again a couple of days after the concert in the park. He'd broken his parole again, going missing for days on end.

'He needs our help,' I said.

'And he's going to get it,' Beccs said, 'whether he likes it or not.'

We smiled, most unlike Frank Fisher, with no nicotine or malevolence on our breath.

***

My mobile bleeped with a voice message coming through after I'd turned it on just after the show. Ray. I listened. Beccs was watching me. Ray talked, I listened, Beccs watched.

'Everything okay?' she asked, noticing the expression on my face as I clicked closed the telephone line.

I nodded. I laughed.

'What's the matter?' she said.

I dialled the messaging system again, handing my mobile to Beccs, sitting back to watch her as she listened. Ray spoke, Beccs listened, I watched, knowing what he had to say:

'Listen.

'You win.

'I know.

'That lad – your lyricist – in nick again. Boy needs a job, yeah?

'You can – if you like – break your contract. Don't know at what cost. All round.

'Or.

'Or. You can work with McGregor and Fine.

'You can have it, you know, your way.

'And.

'And there's – American promoter's seen the vid of the park concert. They love it. Think about it.

'Think about it.

'America.

'Think about it.'

Beccs came off the phone. She thought about it. We looked at each other.

'America?' she said.

We just laughed.

Also by John Brindley

Amy Peppercorn: Starry-eyed and Screaming

Sixteen-year-old Amy Peppercorn has a lot to scream about. Her best friend Beccs is being lured away by that hateful boy beacon, Kirsty. School sucks. Her family are impossible to live with. Know the feeling?

Then – although she SO didn't mean to – she falls under the spell of the cool, irresistible Ben and joins his band. Everything changes.

Because Amy's scream is her fortune. She's going to be a pop sensation and she's on her way.

As John Brindley charts her road to fame there is glitz and excitement. But secrets and startling revelations also unfold in a story that packs a huge emotional punch.

Stardom has its price – how much will Amy pay?

Changing Emma

When Emma's family win £23.5 million on the lottery, Emma gets everything she ever dreamed of. Who needs GCSEs when there's all that money to spend!

Catapulted from her humdrum life with Mum, Dad and Gran, she's up to her neck in champagne parties, designer clothes, swimming pools and spending sprees in Paris and New York. Of course she changes – wouldn't you?

But Emma is seconds away from going under – for ever.

This is the dark side of the fairy tale – a riveting, uncompromising, fast-paced story about what can happen to an ordinary girl when she gets all the money she never knew she wanted.

Rhino Boy

Ryan is an ordinary boy with an ordinary life – until the day he grows a rhinoceros horn in the middle of his forehead.

And now Ryan the school bully knows how it feels to be jeered at and whispered about, he knows what it's like to be the focus of media frenzy. He knows what it does to the mother he sneers at, the sister he snipes at, the father he hardly ever sees. And all Ryan's anger, fear, shame and disillusionment explode.

'fizzes with the pain and rage of a wounded animal – in this case the school-bully son of a deserting dad . . . psychological horror at its best. Brindley's richly imaged writing fairly burns with violence.' *The Times*